Harriet
Spies

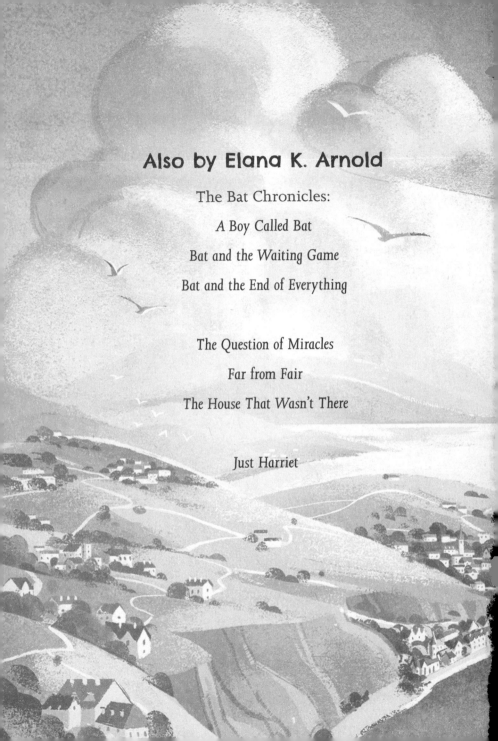

Also by Elana K. Arnold

The Bat Chronicles:

A Boy Called Bat

Bat and the Waiting Game

Bat and the End of Everything

The Question of Miracles

Far from Fair

The House That Wasn't There

Just Harriet

Harriet Spies

Elana K. Arnold
With drawings by Dung Ho

WALDEN POND PRESS
An Imprint of HarperCollinsPublishers

Walden Pond Press is an imprint of HarperCollins Publishers.

Library of Congress Cataloging-in-Publication Data

Names: Arnold, Elana K., author. | Ho, Dung, illustrator.

Title: Harriet spies / Elana K. Arnold ; with drawings by Dung Ho.

Description: First edition. | New York, NY : Walden Pond Press,
    [2023] | Audience: Ages 6-10. | Audience: Grades 2-3. |
    Summary: "Harriet Wermer investigates more mysteries
    during her stay on Marble Island"— Provided by publisher.

Identifiers: LCCN 2022029580 | ISBN 978-0-06-309213-6 (hardcover)

Subjects: CYAC: Mystery and detective stories. | Bed
    and breakfast accommodations—Fiction. | LCGFT:
    Detective and mystery fiction. | Novels.

Classification: LCC PZ7.A73517 Har 2023 | DDC [Fic]—dc23

LC record available at https://lccn.loc.gov/2022029580

Typography by Molly Fehr

22 23 24 25 26 LBC 5 4 3 2 1

First Edition

For Henry, also known as Professor Higglebottom.
Sisses adores you, you wonderful kid.

Contents

1

A Visitor to Marble Island

IF YOU'RE NOT A PEOPLE person, you probably wouldn't like living at a bed-and-breakfast.

(Even if you really like beds, and you really like breakfasts.)

Lucky for me, I am a people person . . . most of the time. I think people are interesting. They look all different sorts of ways, and they do their hair in all different sorts of styles, and they wear all different sorts of outfits. Especially when they are on vacation. And pretty much everyone who comes to my Nanu's Bric-a-Brac B&B on Marble Island is on vacation.

I'm not here on vacation, though. I'm here because my mom back home is pregnant and on bed rest, so she can't look after me, and my dad has to travel for work, so he can't look after me, either. Usually, Nanu's job is to run the B and B, but this summer her job is also to look after me. And my job is to help her with B and B stuff. And also to look after Matzo Ball, the world's best cat.

I guess Nanu's basset hound, Moneypenny, doesn't have a job, unless it's hogging the sunny spot in the front window. She's getting a little better at sharing with Matzo Ball, though.

Actually, I have lots of jobs. Besides helping Nanu with the B and B and taking care of Matzo Ball, I'm also cleaning out Nanu's storage shed and I'm making gingerbread birdhouses with Mabel Marble, the neighbor who lives on the other side of the wall in the backyard. And sometimes I help Hans and Gretchen by tasting new ice cream flavors at their shop (though vanilla is still my favorite).

My goal was to get the back shed all cleaned out before my dad came to visit me. But it had already been two weeks since he'd first brought me to the island and he was arriving today, and with all my other jobs, the shed still hadn't been cleaned out.

Maybe that was better, though. It meant that Dad would be able to help me. Dad likes to be helpful.

After we washed the breakfast dishes, Nanu and I got ready to go pick up Dad from the ferry. I was so excited to see him that I kept doing my Happy to See Dad dance, which I was making up as I went along. Basically it involved lots of spins and dramatic arm movements and things like that.

"If you keep that up," said the Captain, "poor Moneypenny won't ever settle in for her morning nap."

The Captain, a visiting ornithologist to Marble

Island, was Nanu's longest-standing guest at the Bric-a-Brac. (An ornithologist, if you don't know, is a bird expert. And do you know what experts love, more than almost anything else? Talking about the thing they're an expert on. Don't get the Captain going about island loggerhead shrikes if you don't have at least half an hour to listen.) In addition to being Nanu's longest-standing guest, the Captain is also the tallest. And maybe the strongest. Everything about the Captain is impressive. Now she was standing at the bottom of the stairs. She had on her birding vest, with all the little pockets, and her birding hat, with its wide brim, and she wore her binoculars around her neck. She was patting all the pockets of her vest, like she was looking for something.

"Moneypenny already had two naps this morning," I said, which wasn't technically true, but might have been. "She's all napped out."

"Hmm," said the Captain, and she looked like maybe she was going to say something else, but just then Nanu came out of the kitchen carrying a big paper bag—the kind you get from the grocery store—and held it out.

"Here you go, Captain," Nanu said. "There was just enough olallieberry jam left to make your sandwiches. And there's hard-boiled eggs, and a thermos of tea, and fruit, of course."

"Thank you, Agnes," said the Captain. Then she asked, "Have you seen my compass?"

The Captain was one of the smartest people I'd ever met, but she sure did misplace things a lot. Fortunately, Nanu was *great* at finding things. You know that saying, about how someone might lose their head if it wasn't screwed on? I don't think the Captain would ever forget her head, but she forgets most everything else. Except her binoculars. A bird-watcher wouldn't get far without those.

"I found the compass on the dining room table and slipped it into your lunch bag so you wouldn't forget it," Nanu said.

"Ah," the Captain said. "Thank you." She took the lunch bag. It looked heavy.

Nanu picked up her bright-yellow hat from the entry table and pushed it firmly over her curly hair. I like Nanu's hair. I hope that one day when I'm really old mine will be silver and gray and white and brown, like hers.

"Agnes," said the Captain, frowning, "your hat has so much cat hair on it that it's practically meowing." She set her lunch bag on the front table, took the hat from Nanu's head, and, opening the front door, shook it until Matzo Ball's peachy perfect fuzz rose from it in a cloud. "The fusillade of fur is really becoming a problem," she continued. "It gets everywhere. Something needs to change." She handed the hat back to Nanu.

"He barely drops any fur at all," I said, ignoring the Captain's showy big words.

Matzo Ball must have heard us talking about him. Or maybe he just heard the front door opening. Either way, he appeared like a bolt of silent orange lightning and darted outside. He stopped still, all his perfect whiskers pointing forward. Something was rustling around in the front bushes, and Matzo Ball was going to do his best to sneak up on it. He took one silent step forward . . . then another . . .

The Captain's big, square hands reached down and grabbed him, just before he leaped into the bushes. "Oh no, you don't," she said.

"Mrow," said Matzo Ball, insulted.

"He wasn't going to hurt anything," I said. "He was just exploring."

"Tell that to the bird I pried out of his jaws the day before yesterday," said the Captain. She carried Matzo Ball back inside and dropped him unceremoniously on the rug. I could tell from the way he twitched his ears that he was irritated, but he stretched out a leg and began to groom it, pretending that he didn't care at all about the Captain. "Harriet," she said, "I've told you at least half a dozen times that you must keep a better watch on this feline of yours."

I know that "feline" is just a fancy word for "cat," but it was the way the Captain said it that I didn't like. I dropped to my knees and scratched the top of Matzo Ball's head to distract him from the insult. "I always know exactly where Matzo Ball is," I said, which was a lie. It's basically impossible to *always* know where a cat is. They are very particular about their private time.

But the Captain wasn't listening to me. "Agnes," she said to Nanu, "I really do wonder if the cat should be allowed downstairs at all. Between the bird chasing and the shedding and the clawing, it might be better for everyone if he was kept strictly upstairs."

"It wouldn't be better for Matzo Ball." I scooped him onto my lap and squeezed his fuzzy, perfect, peachy body. He began to purr. "It wouldn't be better for *me*." I turned to Nanu. "Tell the Captain that Matzo Ball can go anywhere he wants."

But Nanu didn't. Instead, she said, "The Captain has a point, Harriet. You do need to keep a better eye on him. Cute as Matzo Ball is, his time here hasn't entirely been smooth sailing."

"If it's too much responsibility for Harriet to mind her cat," the Captain said, "maybe Walter could take him back across to the mainland."

There was *no way* I was going to let Dad take my cat away from Marble Island. And what made the Captain think *she* was in charge, anyway? She was just a guest at the bed-and-breakfast! A bossy guest.

"One way or the other," said the Captain, picking up her lunch bag, "something must be done about that cat."

I narrowed my eyes at the Captain's lunch bag. Then I said, "Nanu, did you give the Captain *all* the olallieberry jam? I was saving it for Dad."

"We can stop by the market for a fresh jar." Nanu put her hat back on.

I didn't really want to make jam sandwiches for lunch. I was just mad at the Captain. Sometimes when I'm mad or anxious or bored, I say things that aren't true. It's a bad habit, and one I'm trying to break. But now I had another problem, which was that I didn't want to stop at the market.

"Let's just make egg salad," I said. "I don't want to waste any of my Dad time at the grocery store."

Dad had told me on the phone that he'd only be able to stay for four hours, the time between when the first morning ferry arrived and when the early-afternoon ferry left, so that he could get home to Mom before dinner. The Captain had given me an old watch with a flashlight and a countdown timer on it, and I had it strapped to my wrist, ready to go.

All of us went out of the B and B together after I said goodbye to the pets. Moneypenny was asleep on the window seat, and Matzo Ball was continuing his tongue bath. He was surrounded by a ring of shedding fur, but I ignored it. Nanu put a sign on the door—"Back in a Jiffy!"—and the Captain walked up the street to her Jeep. I wasn't at all sorry to see her go.

Then Nanu and I climbed into her golf cart. Almost everyone who lives on Marble Island drives a golf cart instead of a regular car. The Captain has a Jeep because her job is to study the island loggerhead shrikes, a very important and very specific type of bird, and to do that, she has to drive on the bumpy dirt roads to the middle of the island to observe them. I had been asking her to take me along, but the Captain says I have to practice being quiet for thirty whole minutes—all in a row— before she will. Otherwise, I'll scare off the shrikes. That's what she'd originally given me the watch with the timer for. Practice. So far, the best I'd done was eighteen minutes and twenty-three seconds.

Nanu started up the golf cart and off we went. I was so excited to see Dad I could hardly stand it, but luckily Marble Island is pretty small, and it only took us a few minutes to get to the dock.

The ferry was already there!

"It's early today," Nanu said approvingly. Nanu likes it when things are on time, and she likes it even better when they're early.

I jumped out of the golf cart as soon as it pulled up to the curb. A whole herd of tourists was pouring down the ramp from the ferry—a big mess of strollers and backpacks and hats and parasols and people, some pointing at a pelican who sat on the railing, some staring down at their phones as if whatever they were looking at was more interesting than Marble Island, even though they'd just arrived.

But no Dad.

"Maybe he missed the ferry," I said to Nanu, who had gotten out of the golf cart and stood beside me. "Or maybe," I said, suddenly sick to my stomach, "something is wrong with Mom and he couldn't come at all."

"Or maybe," said Nanu, bending down so our cheeks were side by side, "he's right there."

She pointed, and I looked, and there he was. Blue baseball cap and a big smile. My dad.

I ran through the herd of tourists straight for him. Dad opened his arms and I jumped up, and he caught me.

"Hey there, Harriet." His voice was sort of rough like his cheek. He squeezed me tight for a long time before he set me down, and then he put his big warm hand on my shoulder, right where it belongs.

"Hello, Walter," said Nanu. Dad hugged her, too, and then the three of us made our way back to the golf cart.

Right then, if the Captain had seen me, she would have been surprised. For once, I couldn't have said a word, even if I'd wanted to. Even though I was happy, my throat felt all tight and full, as if a bunch of words were crowding together and blocking the way, like a traffic jam. And not one of them could get through.

Some of the words were happy, but not all of them. I was glad Dad was here, but now that he was, I was also mad that he would be leaving in four hours. I didn't want to feel mad. Nanu says that sometimes you can choose how you feel, but I don't know about that.

I set my timer for four hours and watched as the seconds started ticking away.

I swallowed down the big tangled lump of words. "Come on, Dad." I grabbed his hand and pulled him toward the golf cart. "We can't waste any time!"

2

Time Stops
for No One

THE FIRST THING I DID as soon as we were back at the B and B was I showed my dad the old cardboard box full of the dollhouse stuff he'd crafted when he was a kid, which I'd found in Mabel Marble's basement. I dragged it out from the closet under the stairs and into the sitting room.

"You sit there." I pointed Dad to the rocking chair that the Captain liked to sit in. He sat. "I want to show you all my favorite things that you made, and then I want you to tell me how you made them."

My voice came out kind of bossy, but Dad just said, "Okay!"

The first thing I pulled out of the box was the little tiny armoire. An armoire is like a closet but it's a piece of furniture, not built into a house.

"Ah," said Dad. I handed it to him, and he turned it over. He ran his thumb over the smooth wood. "This was a tricky one. I had to sand down the doors until they were exactly the same size, and I had to wait for three weeks for a special order of tiny hinges. Look," he said, holding it out to me. "Do you see how small these screws are?"

I squinted, but even like that it was hard to see how the screws fit into the hinges.

"When I get home, I'll mail you my magnifying glass," he said. "Then you'll be able to take a closer look."

"You have a magnifying glass?" I hadn't ever seen one lying around. If I had, I would have remembered it. Magnifying glasses are neat.

"Yup! But I haven't used it in a long time."

We went through the whole box together. I think Dad could have sat there all day telling me about all the dollhouse furniture he'd made, and I was having a really good time listening to him, but I kept looking down at my watch and seeing the minutes slipping away. It made me itchy all over, the way time was passing so quickly. At school, four hours was the amount of time between the first bell and the lunch bell, and it always seemed like it took forever, but here on the island, with only four hours to spend with Dad, it hardly seemed like long enough to do anything, let alone everything I had planned.

In my head, I started crossing things off the list:

- A trip to Hans & Gretchen's Ice Cream Parlor

- ~~Taking bread crusts down to the water to feed to the garibaldi~~
- ~~A visit to Mabel Marble on the other side of~~ the gate

I didn't want to share my Dad time with *anyone.*

"Come on," I said, grabbing his hand and pulling him toward the back door. "I want you to help me clean out the rest of the shed."

Dad's hand felt warm and strong. He squeezed mine—once, twice, three times, which means "I love you." I squeezed his hand three times, too.

I'd been working on the shed ever since I got to Marble Island two weeks ago. And I had a lot of it cleared out. There was one big set of shelves on the far wall that was too heavy for me, and some old cans of paint that Nanu had told me not to touch because they might be toxic.

Dad piled the old paint cans by the trash bins and looked up the number for Hazardous Waste

Collection. They said they'd come get the cans on Monday when the rest of the trash was collected.

Then we took a good look at the shelves. "How about instead of taking these out, we give them a good wash?" he suggested. "That way, Nanu will have a place to store her things when she fills the shed up again."

I didn't really want Nanu to fill the shed up with a bunch of junk, after all the work I'd done to get it clean, but shelf space did sound like a good idea. So I got a couple of rags and a bucket and Dad filled it with soapy water and we got to work.

It took nearly an hour to get the shelves clean, but it felt good, working alongside Dad. He whistled the way he did when he was busy and happy, and it reminded me so much of home that I would have started crying if I wasn't so busy scrubbing.

Finally we were done, and Dad said we should leave the door to the shed open to let it all dry out while we ate our lunch.

"It can't be time for lunch already," I said, but I looked at my watch and it was. It was five minutes past noon. More than two hours were gone.

Dad washed up at the kitchen sink while Nanu spooned egg salad onto bread for sandwiches. Even though I didn't want it to be lunchtime already, all the cleaning had made me hungry. Nanu cut the sandwiches into triangles rather than fingers since it would be just the three of us having lunch, no guests. All the people staying at the B and B this week were part of one big group—the Dunston family. They were on Marble Island for a wedding, and they'd be gone until late doing all the weird things people do to get ready for weddings.

For example, before they'd headed out, early, I'd heard the bride's parents talking about needing to find something old, something borrowed, something blue, and something new. They said it like it was part of a tradition or something.

"Well, Carmen's wedding dress is new," Mrs.

Dunston had said. "So we already have that covered."

Weddings seemed like a lot of work for something that's supposed to be fun.

With all the guests out of the house, it was nice to have the B and B just to the three of us today. Before we could have lunch, Nanu balled up the tablecloth—there was kind of a lot of cat fur—and replaced it with a new one. Then we sat together at the dining room table and ate our sandwiches. Nanu asked questions about Mom and the baby, and Dad told us that everything was going just fine but that Mom still wasn't supposed to get out of bed, which meant that Dad was doing all the shopping and cleaning and chores and stuff, which usually he and Mom split fifty-fifty, not to mention all the stuff I did around the house.

"It's awfully quiet without Harriet," Dad said.

"And Matzo Ball," I reminded him.

"And Matzo Ball," he agreed.

"And how about you, Walt? How's your work going?" asked Nanu.

That was going to be boring grown-up stuff, and I was all done with my sandwich, so I went into the sitting room to see what Moneypenny and

Matzo Ball were up to. They were sleeping on the window seat cushion. Matzo Ball was in his kitten position—head tucked between his paws—and one of Moneypenny's long soft ears wrapped over him like a blanket.

"Aww," I said, and I went back to the dining room to tell Dad that he *had* to see the cutest thing.

But he was in the middle of a sentence. "—laid off three people already, and who knows who might be next." He stopped talking when he saw me standing in the doorway, which was perfect timing because I had an important announcement.

"Moneypenny's ears are the perfect size to be a nap blanket for Matzo Ball!"

Nanu and Dad both came to see, and we all stood there and oohed and aahed and Dad snapped a picture to show to Mom when he got home. But that reminded me that Dad would be leaving soon, and we were running out of time.

"I'll take care of the lunch dishes," Nanu said, shooing us out of the kitchen "Why don't you two take a few cookies over to Mabel Marble?"

Dad thought that was a great idea, but I didn't. It's not that I don't love Mabel Marble—I do. It was just that I'd already planned not to share any of my Dad time.

So I said, "Mabel Marble isn't home."

"She isn't?" said Nanu.

I shook my head. "She told me she'd be gone all afternoon."

"Oh," said Nanu. "Well, I suppose you can just leave the cookies on her porch, then." She wrapped six cookies in a cloth napkin and placed them in a little basket.

"Come on, Harriet," Dad said. "You can show me the old key. I still can't believe you found it!"

When I first got to the island, I'd found a key in an old dresser in the shed, and then I'd discovered the gate it opened. I'd been looking forward to showing it to Dad, but now that I'd lied about Mabel Marble not being home, suddenly I didn't want to.

"I don't know where the key is," I said.

The thing about lying is that one lie can lead to another. Sort of like a lie avalanche.

"It's in your pocket, Harriet," Nanu said. "I saw you put it in there this morning."

"Oh." I stuck my fingers into the small pocket on the front of my overalls (where I always kept the key) and I fished it out. "Thank you."

Dad carried the basket and I carried the key, and together we went to the back gate. Dad watched as I stuck the key in the lock and jiggled it. Then it twisted and the gate swung open, into Mabel Marble's wonderful yard.

The grass was still overgrown, but it was a little bit greener since I'd started watering it every afternoon. And there were a few new gingerbread houses in the trees. You could tell the ones I had made from the ones Mabel Marble had made. Mine were crooked and ramshackle, and hers were tall and straight, but Mabel Marble said that they all tasted just as good to the birds.

"Hello, Harriet," called Mabel Marble from the porch, where she sat in a rocking chair. "Hello, Walt! How lovely to see you."

We went up the porch stairs together. Dad bent down to give Mabel Marble a hug. She looked even older and more frail than usual next to my dad.

He gave her the basket of cookies. "I didn't know you were home," Dad said.

"Oh, yes. I rarely go out these days. Most everything I need is right here." Mabel Marble waved her cane, pointing at the trees, the birds, the sky.

"Harriet seemed to believe you were out for the afternoon," said Dad.

I stuck my hands in my pockets and whistled, and I did a little tap dance to distract them. But even though Mabel Marble is almost a hundred years old—her centennial birthday is at the end of the summer—she isn't easily distracted.

"Did she?" Mabel Marble said. "I wonder where she got that impression."

"Mabel Marble," I said loudly. "Tomorrow I'm going to have a yard sale to get rid of all the non-trash stuff I've cleaned out from Nanu's shed!"

I had not been planning on having a yard sale. I made up the yard sale plan right then, to change the subject. But as soon as I'd said it, I decided it actually was a good idea. Sometimes that happened when I lied—I'd say something that wasn't true, but then decide that maybe I could *make* it true.

"I can sell anything you might have that you don't need, if you want," I added, feeling generous.

"A yard sale," said Mabel Marble. "I have a few things I should probably clean out of the house. How about you come by after dinner and we'll see what's what."

We were halfway across the yard before she called, "I'll be home all evening, Harriet, just in case you hear otherwise."

That Mabel Marble. No distracting her.

3

After the Ferry

I ALMOST DIDN'T GO WITH Nanu to drop off Dad at the ferry.

"Matzo Ball will be lonely without me," I said.

But sometimes Nanu doesn't take no for an answer. And when we got to the ferry, I was glad that this was one of those times. It was sad to hug Dad goodbye and watch him climb aboard, but it would have been sadder not to. And he promised to visit again in a couple of weeks, and reminded me that I could call him or Mom any time. "Day or night," he said, kissing the top of my head "I hope the yard sale goes great!" Then he got on the boat.

Nanu and I stood together on the dock and watched the big slow ferry pull out into the ocean. We watched until the boat looked small enough to fit inside the dollhouse at the B and B. That's when I wanted to leave. I didn't want to see the boat disappear, which Nanu seemed to understand.

We went by the ice cream shop for a little treat. Nanu was feeling sorry for me, I could tell, and I was sad, but not as sad as I'd been two weeks ago, when Dad had first brought me to the island. Now I knew that I would be okay here without him and Mom, even if I didn't love it.

And I had a really good idea. Even better than the yard sale idea. And I told Nanu about it as we walked slowly back to the B and B, licking our cones.

"I was thinking," I began.

"You always are," said Nanu.

"So after the yard sale," I went on.

"You mean the yard sale you just this afternoon decided to have?"

I looked up at Nanu. But she wasn't irritated; she was smiling. That's one of Nanu's many good qualities. She's good at handling changes in plans. Actually, that was something that I'm not so good at.

I decided I'd think about that later.

"Yes," I said. "That yard sale."

Nanu nodded and licked a drip of melting ice cream from her cone.

"And you know how the shed is nice and clean now, and how it has real windows and a little door and everything?"

"Indeed," said Nanu.

"Well," I said, "I was thinking that the shed is really too nice just to be a house for a bunch of

32

junk. So I was wondering if maybe I could use the shed. As my own space. Just while I'm here for the summer."

"I think that is an excellent idea," said Nanu.

"You do?"

"I do," said Nanu.

I don't know why, but I had thought it would be hard to convince Nanu to let me use the shed.

"We could set up a table in there for crafts and things," Nanu suggested. "Maybe art supplies."

"And Dad and I scrubbed all the shelves, so we can use those, too."

"Lovely," said Nanu. "And I'll tell you what: any money you make tomorrow at the yard sale, you can use to fix up the shed. How does that sound?"

It sounded great. This yard sale idea I came up with was getting better by the minute. I started imagining all the things I could use the shed for. I could store Dad's dollhouse stuff in there. Maybe

I'd check out that book from the library, the one about making miniatures, and I'd try making some stuff on my own. Maybe I could even set up a little cushion by one of the windows for Matzo Ball so he could also have a spot to himself, no Money-penny allowed.

Back at the B and B, I went into the sitting room to tell Matzo Ball the good news about the shed, but he wasn't there. He must have gone upstairs. In the afternoons, he likes to sit in the window of our bedroom and look out at the birds in Mabel Marble's trees.

The Captain was there, though, sitting in her thinking chair. Her binoculars were on the table next to her. She had her feet up on a footstool and she was reading one of her bird books. The Captain is very good at sitting still. That's a talent I don't have.

There was an extra furry spot on the middle couch cushion, where Matzo Ball must have slept for a while. I sat on it to hide the fur from the Captain, and then I told her about how I was going to fix up the shed as a hangout, and how Nanu told me I could use the money from a yard sale we'd be having tomorrow. "If you have anything you need to sell, I could take care of it," I said. *And add that money to the shed fund,* I didn't say.

But she replied, "I travel light, lass. I didn't bring much to the island beyond my books and binoculars. And they're far too important to sell." She picked up the binoculars from where they sat beside her.

She held them out, and I took them. They were heavy, and they had a really nice strap, black and smooth and cool.

"Careful, lass, they're delicate," the Captain said.

I know how to handle delicate things, and I was a little annoyed that the Captain apparently didn't think so, but I didn't say anything. I just handed back the binoculars, and she set them on the table.

"What makes your binoculars so special, anyway? They just look like regular old binoculars to me."

The Captain cleared her throat. "These were a gift from my father, years ago. He gave them to me when I earned my PhD in ecology."

"Oh." A present from her dad. That was something I could understand. "Well," I said, "if you don't have anything to *sell*, maybe you'll find something you want to *buy*. The yard sale will start bright and early."

The Captain nodded approvingly. She was a morning person.

She rested her hands on the armrests of the chair, and then she frowned. "What's this?" she said.

I looked up at the ceiling and whistled. I already knew what it was. It was the place where Matzo Ball had sharpened his claws.

The Captain shook her head. "Something must be done about that cat," she said, again.

I didn't like the sound of that at all.

Since the Dunstons were all having dinner at a restaurant in town, Nanu and I ate our dinner upstairs in the little apartment. It was small and cozy up there, just right for the two of us. Moneypenny flopped mournfully under the table, hoping for crumbs, and Matzo Ball, ignoring us, batted at the string that hung down from the window shades. He likes to bat at things. It's one of the top ten cutest things about him. I wished the Captain had been there to see it so she would maybe stop being so annoyed with him all the time.

Between her complaints about his shedding and how upset she got whenever Matzo Ball tried to chase a bird, maybe the Captain really *would* try to make me send him home to Mom and Dad. And that was something I would *not* let happen.

After we finished eating, I headed to Mabel Marble's to see what she had for the yard sale. Normally when I visited her to help with birdhouses or just to chat, we sat together on her big back porch, but this time she motioned me to come inside.

I followed her through the back door into the kitchen. It looked a lot like the big kitchen downstairs at the B and B, but it wasn't neat and tidy. There was stuff *everywhere*. Wobbly stacks of plates. Old newspapers, bundled together. A rug, rolled up and leaning against the wall in a corner of the kitchen. Folded-up tablecloths—more tablecloths than there were tables probably on the whole entire island. I didn't know where to look, there was so much stuff.

"Is this *all* for the yard sale?" I asked.

"Oh, no," said Mabel Marble. "Just these things here."

She waved her cane to the corner of the kitchen, where a small wooden box sat. It was an old milk crate. Inside were a few mismatched teacups, a bunch of candles (some half burned), and a few tea towels.

"Are you sure you don't want me to sell anything else?" I asked. "You have loads of stuff."

"Oh, well," said Mabel Marble. She fidgeted with the head of her cane, and looked everywhere but at me. "I don't know about that. It is quite a lot, I suppose, but I wouldn't know where to start. Maybe . . ." She went over to the counter and picked up a little glass figurine. It was a ballet dancer. For a minute I thought she was going to add it to the box of stuff, but then she set it down.

"I think that's everything for now," she said.

So I took the box of stuff and said, "Thank you,

Mabel Marble," and then I headed toward the B and B. I turned when I got to the gate, and I saw Mabel Marble looking at me through the kitchen window. She waved. I propped up the box with my knee and waved back.

It was sort of sad, in a way, thinking of Mabel Marble all alone in that big old house full of all that stuff. I wasn't really sure how to feel about that.

I'd think about it later. Right then, I had to get ready.

4

The Yard Sale

"YARD SALE, YARD SALE, YARD sale," I said as soon as I woke up. I'd set the alarm on the watch the Captain had given me to seven a.m. before putting it on my bedside table last night, but I woke up before it went off. Matzo Ball, asleep on the pillow next to my head, yawned. He stuck out his barbed pink tongue. His teeth were sharp and white.

"Today is yard sale day, Matzo Ball," I told him, but Matzo Ball wasn't impressed. He tucked into kitten position and went back to sleep.

I jumped up and got dressed. Getting dressed is easy when you wear the same thing every day, and ever since I'd found them in the closet, I'd been wearing my dad's old overalls from when he was a kid on Marble Island. Someone once told me that Albert Einstein wore the same outfit every day so that he wouldn't have to think about clothes, and he could spend more time thinking about science stuff. If it's good enough for Albert Einstein, it's good enough for me, Harriet Wermer.

Another good thing about overalls—besides how easy they are to put on and how comfortable they are—is all the pockets. Just like always, I put the key to the gate in the front middle pocket. I put spare change in the left side pocket in case I needed it for the yard sale. And I still had, like, four empty pockets! Why anyone would wear anything other than overalls is a mystery to me. After strapping the Captain's old watch to my right wrist, I was ready to go.

Downstairs, Nanu was taking fresh muffins out of the oven. That is one of the best things about spending the summer at the Bric-a-Brac B&B: Nanu's morning muffins. There was coffee in the pot (blech!) and tea in the kettle (meh) and hot chocolate ready to be poured into cups (yum).

"Good morning, Harriet," Nanu said.

"*Great* morning, you mean," I said.

"*Great* morning," Nanu agreed. "Have a muffin."

I took a muffin and went into the sitting room. There was the box Mabel Marble had given me, sitting on the table by the front window. There were some other boxes, too, stuff Nanu had pulled off of shelves and out of closets that she didn't need anymore. First I hauled Nanu's folding table out to the front lawn, and then it took another three trips to get all the stuff outside.

Then I was ready for business. But what's funny is that sometimes even if you're ready for something to start, the rest of the world isn't, not always.

Sometimes you have to let the world know what you're doing if you want people to pay attention.

"Yard sale!" I yelled, as loud as I could. "Yard sale! Come and get it!"

The Captain poked her head out of her bedroom window, on the second floor. "Harriet," she said, "it is not yet seven thirty in the morning. I'd wager not all the neighbors want to be woken quite this early, even by your dulcet tones."

I didn't know what "dulcet" meant, but I got the main idea. "How am I going to get customers, then?" I said.

"Have you hung signs?" asked the Captain.

I hadn't. It was a good idea.

"Also," said the Captain, "I couldn't find my binoculars last night. Have you seen them?"

"They're on the table in the sitting room," I said, and then I went to get stuff to make signs.

The Captain was right. She usually is, I guess. As soon as I got the signs posted—one on the corner and another hanging on the windshield of Nanu's golf cart, which was sitting next to the front walkway right where people could see it on their morning strolls—customers started coming by.

First was Hans and Gretchen. They were on their way to the ice cream shop.

"Do you have any kitchen equipment?" Gretchen asked. I pointed her to the box at the end of the table, full of stuff Nanu had pulled out of her cabinets and drawers. Gretchen held up a scooper. "How much for this?"

"Seventeen dollars," I said. I like the number seventeen.

"Ho, ho!" said Hans. "That's a little rich for our blood. How about fifty cents?"

"It's an antique," I said.

"I'll give you one dollar," said Gretchen, "and a free scoop of ice cream next time you come into the shop."

"Deal." I took the dollar and put it in my pocket,

and Gretchen took the scooper. "I'll come by later for the ice cream," I called as they headed down the street toward town. Yard sales are hungry work. I was looking forward to the ice cream already.

Then it got really busy.

The family who was staying at the B and B came outside—Mr. and Mrs. Dunston, who were the parents of the bride, and their younger kids, Lilliam and Frank, who looked like teenagers. The one who was getting married, Carmen, was probably getting her beauty sleep. An old granddad-looking fellow was with them, too. His name was also Mr. Dunston, but he said everyone called him Senior, because he was the oldest, I guess. He was staying in the main floor guest room because stairs were hard for him. He came slowly down the ramp and then across to where my yard sale tables were set up.

"An entrepreneur," he said approvingly.

I shrugged.

"Do you know what that means?" he asked.

"Yes," I said, even though I didn't. I don't know why I lied. It wasn't like it mattered if I knew what "entrepreneur" meant. I was trying really hard to quit lying, but bad habits are hard to break.

"It means you're a self-starter," Senior said. "A go-getter."

"I know," I said. Then, "Do you want to buy anything?"

"You see, Frank?" Senior said to his grandson, who was waiting over on the sidewalk. "This is what I'm talking about!"

Frank sighed. I got the feeling that Senior was the sort of person who really liked to tell other people how they should do things.

Frank's sister Lilliam said, "We're looking for something blue. Do you have anything blue?"

I remembered Mrs. Dunston yesterday saying that they needed something blue, probably for the

wedding. Digging through one of the boxes, I found a big blue tablecloth. I felt a little twinge of regret; it used to be one of Nanu's very favorite tablecloths, but Matzo Ball had chewed off half the little velvet dingle balls that used to be attached to its hem, and I guess Nanu decided the B and B couldn't use it anymore. Sometimes Matzo Ball is a little naughty.

Lilliam shook her head. "That's too big," she said, and she walked away.

Well. She hadn't said *anything* about size! Just color.

Senior was still digging through the boxes, but the rest of the Dunstons seemed ready to leave.

"Come on, Senior," Frank said.

Senior shrugged his shoulders at me, and I shrugged mine.

It was quiet for a while, and I filled the time by practicing my whistle. That was something the Captain was really good at—whistling. When the

Captain whistled, it sounded like a bright, crisp blast. Probably if I asked her to show me how to do it, she would. But I didn't want her help. I put my lips together and blew. Out came a little wet sound like a floppy whisper. I practiced until Jamal, the island's librarian, came by. He was with someone who looked a lot like him, only shorter. They had the same tall hair and the same round glasses and the same deep-brown skin.

"Hey, Jamal," I said. "Do you want to buy some stuff?"

"Hello, Harriet," Jamal answered. "I don't know if I need any stuff, but I do want to introduce you to my little brother. He's about your age. Clarence, this is Harriet. Harriet, this is Clarence."

"Hi," I said to Clarence. Then I asked, "So you live on Marble Island all year long?"

But Clarence didn't look very interested in conversation. "How much for this box of stuff?" he asked. He was pointing to Mabel Marble's box.

"Five dollars," I said. I was getting tired of having a yard sale and was ready to make some deals.

Clarence reached into his pocket and pulled out a wrinkly five-dollar bill. He handed it to me. Then he took the box and headed up the street. He didn't even say goodbye.

"Clarence!" Jamal called. "Don't you want to get to know Harriet? I'll bet she could use a friend on the island!"

"That's okay," I said to Jamal. "I have Matzo Ball and Nanu and Mabel Marble and Moneypenny. I don't need any more friends."

Jamal looked like he was going to say something else, but then Clarence turned the corner and disappeared, and I guess Jamal decided he needed to catch up with him. "Come by the library anytime, Harriet," he said over his shoulder, and then he waved goodbye and disappeared around the corner, too.

That's when the Captain finally came outside. She looked unhappy. But the Captain looks unhappy a lot, even when she's happy. That's just the way her face is made.

"Harriet," she said, "I didn't see my binoculars on the table. Are you sure you didn't move them?"

"One hundred percent sure," I said.

I wasn't actually 100 percent sure. I was more like 93 percent sure. I couldn't think of a time when I would have moved them between yesterday and this morning; I'd been getting ready for the yard sale the whole time. But it's not like I remembered what I was doing every single second.

Maybe the Captain could tell by my face or my voice that I wasn't as sure as I said I was. Her face got a little more unhappy. But it wasn't my fault the Captain was always misplacing her things. I stared back at her until she headed inside. "Maybe I left them on the back porch," I heard her say to herself.

My stomach rumbled. So far all I'd had was a muffin and a cup of hot chocolate, and I was ready for something more "substantial," as Nanu liked to say. I wondered if maybe there was some leftover egg salad. I counted the money in my pocket. I had thirty-four dollars and thirteen cents, which felt like a good place to stop, since thirty-four is seventeen times two.

I got my pen and flipped over the "YARD SALE" sign.

"EVERYTHING FREE," I wrote. Then I dragged the half-empty boxes to the curb and I went inside.

5

What Happened
to Moneypenny

"THEY AREN'T ON THE TABLE and they aren't
in my room and they aren't on the back porch,"
the Captain was telling Nanu, who was bustling
around the kitchen. It was going to be a busy day
for Nanu because the Dunston family was going
to host a party at teatime for the other people who
had come to the island for Carmen's wedding. Most
everyone else was staying at the big hotel in town,
but the Dunstons liked the idea of having "a homey

gathering" at the Bric-a-Brac before the official rehearsal dinner.

Nanu being so busy meant that she didn't have time to help the Captain look for her missing binoculars, and it also meant that I had to make my own egg salad sandwich. And it *also* meant that Nanu didn't have time to take Moneypenny for her constitutional, which is just a fancy word for a walk.

After I made my sandwich and ate it, I got Moneypenny all harnessed up. The Captain was still rattling around the dining room, looking for her binoculars and probably more food to eat. Moneypenny and I went onto the front porch. I was surprised to see that the boxes with the extra yard sale stuff had already disappeared. I wondered who had taken them, and hoped they'd enjoy whatever random stuff they found inside.

This time, I *did* have to use the little plastic bag to clean up after Moneypenny (blech!), right out front of Mabel Marble's house.

Do you know how you can look at something a hundred times and never notice it until one day you do? Well, that happened to me when I finished tying the little bag. What I noticed was this: all of Mabel Marble's windows, upstairs and downstairs, were dusty and dirty. They looked like they hadn't been washed in maybe my whole lifetime. Maybe the reason I noticed was that Nanu is kind of a stickler for clean windows, and because the window seat was Moneypenny and Matzo Ball's favorite hangout, that window was always getting sticky and dirty from their wet noses and foggy breath, and Nanu had made cleaning it one of my chores.

If the Bric-a-Brac B&B's windows were anywhere near as dirty as Mabel Marble's, Nanu would throw a fit. I wondered why they were so dirty, and decided I'd ask Mabel Marble next time I saw her.

"Arf!"

I looked down. Moneypenny was staring at me sternly, like I'd forced her to climb a mountain or something, when all I'd done was take her on a little walk around the block. But maybe I'd feel that way, too, if my legs were three inches long.

"Okay, Moneypenny," I told her. "Let's go home."

"Home" was one of Moneypenny's favorite words, right up there with "bacon." She did her version of a run, which was just a little bit faster than her walk, and eventually we made it back to the B and B.

The Captain was waiting for us on the porch. She had her arms folded across her chest, and she looked even unhappier than before.

"Harriet," she said, "what did you do with all the things you didn't sell?"

"I took them to the curb and put a 'FREE' sign on them," I said.

"Ah," said the Captain. "And what was in those boxes?"

The ones that were left over had all been filled with things Nanu and I had collected. "Stuff from around the B and B."

"And is it possible that something from around the B and B that wasn't intended for sale ended up in those boxes? Like, for example, a pair of binoculars?"

I wanted to say that it wasn't possible. But I had to think about it. So I bent down and untangled Moneypenny from her harness and the leash, trying to remember if there was any chance that the Captain's binoculars could have been in one of the boxes. There had been some old kitchen stuff from Nanu. There had been a lot of stuff from the piles I'd cleared out of the shed, like some small picture frames and old videotapes and toy cars and that sort of thing. Then Nanu had taken a quick look around the B and B and tossed a bunch of things into the boxes last night, like the tablecloth and some candleholders and a doorstop and stuff like that.

There hadn't been any binoculars. I was almost sure of it. And I could see the Captain was really upset, which meant she needed to know how almost-sure I was.

"Captain," I said, "there was some kitchen stuff and some shed stuff and some other odds and ends. But there weren't any binoculars. I would have noticed the binoculars if they had been in one of the boxes."

"Harriet," said the Captain, "I want to believe you. But you don't have the best track record of telling the truth."

Well, this made me mad, that the Captain didn't believe me. And it also made me sad and kind of embarrassed. I don't like feeling mad. But I really don't like feeling sad and embarrassed. So I stomped my foot and yelled, "You're mean and you're wrong and I don't like you."

It wasn't true. I like the Captain. And she's not mean—she's just strict. And she wasn't wrong not to trust me—her reason was sort of a good one, even if it hurt my feelings. And maybe if I'd had a minute to calm down, we would have worked things out there and then. But the thing that happened was that when I stomped my foot, I stomped down right on top of Moneypenny's paw!

Oh, Moneypenny made such a terrible sound. I didn't know a dog could make a sound like that.

"Moneypenny, I'm sorry! It was an accident!" I cried.

Nanu heard poor old Moneypenny's yelp all the way from inside the B and B, and she rushed out, a washcloth in her hands. "What happened to Moneypenny?"

"The lass lost her temper and squashed Moneypenny's paw," the Captain said, which made it sound like I had done it on *purpose*.

"I did *not*!" I yelled. But everyone knew I was lying. Nanu knew it. The Captain knew it. I knew it. Even Moneypenny knew it.

Before anyone could say anything else, I ran inside. I ran up the stairs to the second floor, where the guest rooms were, and up the other set of stairs to the third floor. I ran all the way into my room, the one with the little plaque on the door that read

"Harriet's Hideaway." I slammed the door so hard that the plaque fell off. I heard it thump onto the hallway floor.

Matzo Ball was on my bed, and I buried my face into his soft peachy fur. I would tell you that I didn't cry, but that would be a lie.

6

Not the Boy
Who Cried Wolf

I WASN'T EVER GOING TO come out of my room. That was for sure. I wasn't.

Not even when Nanu knocked on my door to tell me that Moneypenny's paw was just fine, and to ask me if I wanted to come down to see for myself.

Not even when Matzo Ball left to go use his litterbox.

Not even when it was time for the Dunstons' pre–rehearsal dinner get-together, and everyone was downstairs having a good time.

Never, ever.

But then, later, Nanu knocked on my door again. "There's a phone call for you," she said. "It's your mom."

The truth is, by the time Mom called, I was pretty bored in my room. I'd stared out the window and counted all the birds in Mabel Marble's trees; I'd flipped through the library books on my nightstand and read some of each one; I'd crawled under the bed and wondered if anyone would even notice if I just disappeared. And I was hungry. I'd been trying to figure out a way that I could come out of my room without making a big deal about it. A call from Mom was the perfect solution.

I went down all the stairs and into the kitchen. The old-fashioned pink phone was there, waiting for me.

"Hi, Mom," I said. I wound the pink cord around my finger.

"Hello, sweetie. I hear from Nanu that you're having a bad day."

I nodded. But Mom couldn't see that, so I said, "Yes."

"You spent the whole afternoon in your room?"

"Uh-huh."

"That makes two of us," Mom said.

"You *have* to stay in your bed," I said. "You're on bed rest."

"Exactly," said Mom. "But if I *didn't* have to, you can bet I'd be doing all sorts of interesting things."

I nodded again, even though she still couldn't see. I was starting to understand what Mom was hinting at.

"Harriet," said Mom, "half a day stuck in your room is plenty. Go do some things. For me. Okay?"

"Okay," I said.

After we hung up, I wandered into the dining room. Nanu was stacking silverware back into the mahogany, velvet-lined box. I felt bad that I'd missed the whole party. Nanu probably could have used my help.

"Do you want me to put away the rest of the silverware?" I offered.

"Thank you, Harriet. That would be lovely."

One by one, I placed the pieces of silverware back into the box. I liked how the spoons fit together. I worked on the silverware, and Nanu dried the teacups so they could go back into the cabinet. It was nice to be together, working side by side.

"The Captain doesn't believe that I don't know anything about her binoculars," I said suddenly. I hadn't known I was going to say it until I did.

"Ah," said Nanu, nodding. She placed a teacup onto the sideboard shelf.

"Is she really going to stay at the B and B all summer?" I asked. "Maybe she could go live somewhere else."

"Mm," said Nanu, placing another teacup on the shelf. Then she said, "I'll bet you've heard the story of the boy who cried wolf."

I had. That dumb story is about a kid who kept saying he saw a wolf when he really didn't, and the villagers kept running out to help him, but after a while they got tired of his lies, and then a wolf really *did* come, and no one believed him. And then the wolf ate him.

But I didn't see what that story had to do with *me*.

"I didn't say I saw a wolf," I said.

"Yes," said Nanu. "But, Harriet, you *do* have something of a reputation for not always telling the truth."

"That's *different*," I said, even though I wasn't entirely sure *how* it was different. It just *was*. "I'm not lying about the binoculars."

"I believe you," said Nanu.

"And anyway, *she's* the one who's always forgetting where she put things."

"Mm-hmm." Nanu put away the last teacup. I closed the silverware box and put it back in the cabinet. "Follow me," she said. "I want to show you something."

We went into the sitting room. Moneypenny and Matzo Ball were napping in a sunny patch, on the window seat. "Remember when you first

arrived, how Matzo Ball and Moneypenny had to work things out?"

I nodded. "Moneypenny didn't want to share her spot."

"Yes," said Nanu. "And also, Matzo Ball didn't always try to make room for himself in the most polite way he could have."

I knew what Nanu was hinting at—that the Captain was like Moneypenny, and I was like Matzo Ball, and that we would have to work things out, too, same as the pets. And usually, I would like to be compared to Matzo Ball. He is the cutest kitty in the entire universe. But right now, I didn't feel like being taught a lesson. Not even if it involved Matzo Ball.

"Well," I said, "I don't think the Captain is much of a fan of Matzo Ball, even if he and Moneypenny are getting along." What I didn't say was that I also wasn't sure if the Captain was much of a fan of me, and that I wasn't sure anymore how I felt about *her*, either.

But thinking about that gave me an idea. "Nanu," I said, "I'm going to find out what happened to the Captain's binoculars, and I'm going to get them back. Then the Captain will have to apologize for not believing me. And maybe she'll see that if she's wrong about me, she's wrong about Matzo Ball, too."

"Oh, Harriet," Nanu said. "What you need to know about the Captain is—"

"I'm going out to the backyard," I said, interrupting Nanu. I didn't want to hear anything else about the Captain.

I was going to solve the Captain's mystery.

And then I'd decide whether or not to forgive her.

7

Treasure Box

I HEADED FOR MY SHED. Now that it was all cleared out, it was a good place for sitting and thinking. There was a wicker chair that we'd kept, and I put a folded-up blanket on it for a cushion, and I positioned it so I could see out of the shed's open door but no one from the house could see me inside. Then I sat. The chair was wide enough that I could sit cross-legged.

Even though Nanu and the Captain hadn't been

able to find the binoculars, it was possible that they had been misplaced and were still inside some-where. I'd told the Captain that I was 100 percent sure that I didn't have anything to do with her lost binoculars . . . but the more I thought about it, the more I was only, like, 70 percent sure that they hadn't ended up in any of the yard sale boxes. Nanu had been picking up things and putting them into the boxes the night before, and it wasn't like I'd checked what was inside all of them. And then there was the fact that there had been plenty of people going in and out of the B and B since the Captain last saw her binoculars. So it was possible they had been taken by someone else, either by accident or on purpose.

In my head, I made a list of everyone who could have the binoculars:

- Anyone who picked up the boxes of extra stuff that I'd pulled to the curb
- Clarence, who'd bought a box of things for five dollars

- Anyone staying at the B and B
- The Captain, who could have misplaced them inside the B and B

There was no way for me to know who had picked up the boxes of extra stuff, so I set that thought aside for now. Second on my list was Clarence. He had bought a big box of stuff that I hadn't looked at closely, and he'd been very quick to pay five dollars for whatever was inside. Maybe that was because there was something worth a lot more than five dollars in the box.

I needed to find Clarence.

And so I went back inside, where Nanu was still in the dining room, replacing the tablecloth. But she didn't know where Clarence and Jamal lived.

"It's a small island, Harriet, but not that small. I've never been to their house." She paused for a moment. "But do you know who might know . . . ?"

I held up my hand. "Don't say the Captain," I said.

"The Captain," said Nanu, smiling. "Jamal and Clarence's parents oversee the Marble Island Conservancy."

"What's the Marble Island Conservancy?" I asked.

"It's the group that protects and restores the island's natural habitats and endangered species. They keep track of the wild animals and help educate Marble Island residents and visitors about how to respect and protect them. Like the island loggerhead shrikes, for instance."

Those were the birds that the Captain was studying. "So does that mean that Jamal and Clarence's parents are the Captain's bosses?"

"Yes, I suppose it does," said Nanu. "Dr. Williams—their mother—is the director of conservation, and Dr. Hart—their father—is the director of education. So Dr. Williams is the Captain's boss."

I liked the thought of someone telling the Captain what to do and judging how good or bad she was at her job. But I didn't like the idea of asking the Captain for information right then.

"Nanu," I said, "can we go to the library when it opens tomorrow?"

"Of course," she said. "Are you ready to check out some new books?"

"Yes," I said. Which was the truth. But maybe not all of the truth.

It was lucky for me that Jamal was working at the library the next day.

He was pushing a metal cart down the aisles, putting books on shelves. It looked sort of fun.

"Hello, Harriet," he said when I stepped in front of the cart, blocking the aisle. "Can I help you find something?"

"Yes," I said. "Actually, I want you to help me

find someone. Your brother. Clarence."

"Ah!" Jamal smiled. "I was hoping the two of you would become friends. I think you have a lot in common."

I didn't want to find Clarence to become his friend. I wanted to find Clarence to find out what had been in the box I'd sold him for five dollars. But I decided this information was on a need-to-know basis. And Jamal didn't need to know.

"Yep," I said. "Do you know where I can find him?"

"He's at our house," Jamal said. "I can give you the address, if you want."

Sometimes, it's hard to get what you want. But sometimes, it's easy.

Nanu and I walked back to the B and B, and then I left her to head two streets over, to 43 Aster Place, where Clarence, Jamal, and their parents lived.

It was a small, neat house, one story tall with a flat roof and an orange front door and long horizontal wood slats across the front. It looked cool and modern, totally different from the Bric-a-Brac B&B, which was tall and colorful and pointy.

I knocked on the door. After a minute, Clarence answered.

He pushed his glasses up his nose. "Hello," he said.

"Hi," I answered. "I'm Harriet. From the yard sale?"

"I remember," said Clarence. But he didn't scoot to the side to let me in. "Do you need something?"

Right then I decided that the best way to find out if the Captain's binoculars had been in the box I sold to Clarence wasn't to ask him. If I had bought a box of stuff at a yard sale and then the person who sold it to me showed up at my front door asking what was in the box, I probably wouldn't tell them. Why would I? They would maybe be trying to get something back (which was exactly what I was doing).

So instead of asking about the box, I said, "Wanna hang out?"

Clarence blinked. I liked the way his glasses made his eyes look extra big. "Okay," he said. And then he opened the door and let me come inside.

It was nice and cool inside Clarence's house. The air was cool, but the house was also cool, in the other meaning of the word.

Nanu's B and B is comfy cozy and stuffed full of polished antique furniture and rugs and doilies everywhere. Clarence's house had smooth polished concrete floors, and wood paneling, and neat low wood and leather furniture, and tables with nothing on them, and the whole back wall was windows and a big glass door looking out on the back garden.

"Whoa," I said.

"My parents are really into mid-century modern," Clarence said, shrugging. "Leave your shoes by the door, okay?"

I didn't know what mid-century modern was, but I liked it. I kicked off my shoes and lined them up neatly next to the other shoes—a pair of big hiking boots, a smaller pair of hiking boots, a pair of leather sandals, and sneakers that looked about the same size as my shoes, which probably belonged to Clarence.

"Hon, who was at the door?" came a lady's

voice, and then from around the corner came the lady. She was drying her hands on a dishcloth. She wore a light summer dress and had bare feet. Her toenails were painted pearly pink. Her hair was in lots of braids and the braids were coiled together into a bun on the top of her head. "Oh, hello," she said when she saw me.

"Hi," I said. "I'm Harriet."

"Like Harriet the Spy," she said, smiling.

I shook my head. "No," I said, even though it was true that my mother had named me after that character in a book. "It's just Harriet."

I braced myself for Clarence's mom to say, "Well, hello, Just Harriet," the way grown-ups usually did. I don't know why they all thought that was so funny. But instead, she nodded and said, "Hello, Harriet. It's very nice to meet you. I'm Joy."

I decided right there and then that I liked Clarence's mom.

"Are you new to the island?" she asked.

I told her about how my mom was on bed rest and my dad had to travel for work and how I was spending the summer with my grandmother who owns the Bric-a-Brac B&B, and how I'd even brought my cat, Matzo Ball, along with me. I told her about the shed in the backyard and how I'd cleaned it out and how I'd had a yard sale and how Jamal and Clarence had come to the yard sale and how that's where I met Clarence. I *almost* told her about the missing binoculars, but I stopped myself just in time.

Then Joy asked Clarence, "Is *that* where you bought that box of stuff?"

Clarence nodded.

"What a find," Joy said, smiling. "Lots of treasure in that box. Well, Harriet, it's nice to meet you."

Then Clarence said, "C'mon. I'll show you my room."

I followed him down the hallway. But all I could

think about was what Joy had said—Lots of treasure in that box.

If the Captain's binoculars had been in there, now was my chance to find them. I just had to figure out a way to get them back.

8

In Clarence's Room

CLARENCE'S BEDROOM DOOR WAS CRACKED
open. He pushed it open the rest of the way. He
went inside, but I stood in the doorway and stared.

"Whoa."

The rest of the house was sleek and clean and
had empty tables and shelves with just a couple
things on them. But Clarence's room was the opposite.

"What a mess," I said before I could stop myself
from saying it. I clapped my hand over my mouth,

but the words were already out. For a second I thought maybe Clarence would get so mad at me for being rude that he'd make me leave.

But Clarence didn't look upset at all. He pushed his glasses up his nose and said, "It's not a mess. A mess is a place where you don't know where anything is. This is the opposite of that."

I looked around again. And I saw that Clarence was right. Even though his room was packed full of stuff, it didn't look like a random mishmash of things. Everything, it seemed, was in its place.

The big wall had a tall, long set of shelves, all along it. Starting from the bottom, Clarence's shelf held:

- Baskets full of things to build with, like Legos and wooden blocks and Lincoln Logs and magnetic tiles and marble run stuff.
- Books. Lots of them. And they were organized like at a real library, with

colored dots taped onto their spines.

- Science stuff. There was a micro-
  scope and a bunch of slides and a
  model of the solar system and a
  globe that lit up.
- Plants! Like sixteen of them!
- Model cars, all lined up, from biggest to smallest.

And there was a lot more, too, but by the time my eyes reached the third shelf from the top, there was only one thing he had that I cared about:

The Captain's binoculars. There they were, tucked between a camera and a gadget that I'd never seen before.

I went straight for them. I was reaching to pull them from the shelf when Clarence said, "Stop!"

"I wasn't going to touch anything," I said, and I shoved my hands in my pockets.

"There's lots of delicate stuff on my shelves," Clarence said in a softer voice.

"I know how to hold stuff without breaking it," I said. He was reminding me of how the Captain talked to me, which I did not like. "And anyway, I wasn't going to touch anything."

We stood there for a minute, me with my hands in my pockets, Clarence twisting his hands in front of him. He looked as nervous and uncomfortable as I felt. Normally if someone talked to me in a mean voice or a yelling voice or anything like that, I'd let them know what I thought about it. Maybe I'd yell louder or talk meaner, or maybe I'd leave. And part of me wanted to do that right now.

But the bigger part wanted to find out about the binoculars, which meant I needed to stay. I rocked back on my heels. "So," I said, as casually as I could, "where'd you get all this stuff?"

Clarence shrugged. "Some of it was presents. Some is old stuff from my parents' research. Some of it I bought at thrift stores and secondhand shops and—"

"Yard sales?"

Clarence nodded. "Uh-huh. Yard sales can be great places to find cool things."

"What do you do with all this stuff?" I asked, looking back at the shelves, trying not to look too hard at the binoculars.

"I do different stuff with different things." He pointed at the bottom shelf: "Build." The next shelf: "Read." The next shelf: "Experiments." The plants: "Water." The binoculars and other gadgets: "Bird-watching."

"Bird-watching?" I said. "We have someone staying at the bed-and-breakfast who does bird-watching. Bird counting, actually."

Clarence nodded. "I know. Sometimes she comes over here for lunch with my mom."

"She does?" It felt weird to imagine the Captain sitting at someone else's table. "She has the biggest appetite of anyone I've ever met."

"I know!" said Clarence, and his face broke into

a big bright smile. "Last time she came over we ran out of bread."

Then I was smiling, too.

After that, it was a lot easier to talk to Clarence. We compared all the stuff we'd seen the Captain eat—"Once, I saw her eat six hard-boiled eggs," I told him—and we settled onto the carpet and Clarence pulled out a bin of magnetic tiles and we worked side by side on building things.

He didn't try to mess with the thing I was building, or offer advice about how I should be doing it differently, or anything like that. And another thing: he was fair about dividing up the magnetic tiles. Not everyone is fair. And I liked the way he kept pushing his glasses up his nose when they slipped.

"We had a magnet set like this in my classroom last year," I said.

Clarence nodded to show that he was listening, but he didn't look up from the thing he was

building. Lots of the tiles were triangle-shaped, and he was using them to make sails on the base he'd created, which I could now tell was a boat.

"This girl Julia told all the kids that building toys were for babies," I continued. "And then almost no one in the class wanted to play with them anymore."

"Well," said Clarence, "it sounds like Julia doesn't want to be an architect or an engineer."

"Do you want to be an architect or an engineer?"

He shrugged.

I decided then that I liked Clarence.

He put the final triangle piece on his boat. It was sort of a masterpiece, and I noticed he'd used every one of his pieces. There were still a bunch of mine that I didn't know what to do with.

"Show me how you made your boat," I said, taking apart my creation.

"Okay," said Clarence. And he did.

I felt so comfortable there with Clarence that I almost forgot about the binoculars . . . but not quite. I kept sneaking glances up at the shelf, trying to figure out a way to get my hands on them.

Finally, I just asked. "Hey, can I see your binoculars?"

Clarence hesitated, considering. Then he said, "Okay, but be careful. My mom gave them to me for my birthday last year."

Well, after he said that, I didn't really need to hold the binoculars anymore. I guess Clarence could see the disappointment on my face because he asked, "What's the matter?"

I don't know why I decided to tell Clarence the truth right then. But I did.

I told him about the Captain's missing binoculars. I told him how she thought I had misplaced them and maybe accidentally sold them or given them away at the yard sale. I told him that I'd come over here hoping to find them in the box of stuff I'd sold him.

When I finished talking, I looked at his face. It was half closed, half open, like a door.

"What's the matter?" I asked.

"So, you came over here looking for binoculars? You didn't really want to hang out with me?"

I had hurt Clarence's feelings. And it would have hurt my feelings, too, if I thought someone wanted to be my friend, but they were actually just using me for some other reason.

"I'm sorry," I said. "But that was before I knew you. Maybe we could be friends anyway?"

Clarence didn't say anything right away. He

blinked, and his glasses made his eyes extra big.

Finally, he said, "Okay."

I couldn't help it. I smiled. "Good."

"And I'll help you find the Captain's binoculars."

"You will?"

Clarence nodded. "Now that you can eliminate me as a suspect—you don't still think I have the binoculars, do you?"

I shook my head.

"So if I don't have the binoculars, that means someone else does. Is there anyone staying at the bed-and-breakfast right now?"

"Yes," I said. "A whole big family." I told him about my list of people who could have the binoculars, specifically the third item on the list: someone staying at the B and B.

"Okay," said Clarence, nodding. "Let's investigate."

9

Harriet and Clarence the Spies

THE DUNSTONS WEREN'T AT THE bed-and-breakfast.

"They're out and about," Nanu told us when Clarence asked her where they were. "Why do you want to know?"

I tried to shoot Clarence a look that said that's-on-a-need-to-know-basis-and-Nanu-doesn't-need-to-know, but he didn't seem to catch it.

"Harriet thinks maybe one of them might have taken the Captain's binoculars. Her top suspect is

Frank, but she said she wouldn't rule out Senior, either."

"Oh, Harriet," Nanu said.

"I don't think they *stole* them," I said. "I think maybe one of the Dunstons *borrowed* them and forgot to put them back." And then, because the cat was already out of the bag—which was a pretty terrible phrase, now that I was thinking about it—I added, "I just want to ask them a few questions."

"You are not allowed to interrogate the guests," Nanu said. "It's bad for business."

I made fists out of my hands inside my pockets. "But Nanu—"

"No 'but Nanus,'" Nanu said firmly. "This is a hard rule. No interrogating the guests. Do you promise?"

I hated making promises. Because even though I sometimes don't remember to tell the truth, I *never* break a promise. So I try to avoid making them.

But Nanu wasn't letting us go anywhere until

I promised. She reminds me of my dad that way. So I said, "Fine. I promise I won't interrogate the guests."

This seemed to satisfy Nanu. She nodded, and then wiped her hands down her skirt, like she was dusting off the problem. "Good," she said. "Now, who would like a cookie?"

Clarence raised his hand.

"You don't have to raise your hand, Clarence," I said grumpily.

"I think it's charming," said Nanu, and she gave us two cookies each, still warm from the oven.

We ate them on the front porch. Some island brochures were on the table next to the porch chairs: one for glass-bottomed boats and another for kayak rentals. And, on one of them, someone had written a short list of words: "Old," "New," "Borrowed," "Blue." "New" had a checkmark next to it.

It was that list of things I'd heard the Dunstons

talking about the last couple of days. I showed it to Clarence.

"I know about this," he said, taking the brochure. "It's a wedding tradition. When she gets married, the bride is supposed to have something old, and something new, and something borrowed, and something blue. For luck."

"Why blue?" I asked.

Clarence didn't know the answer to that.

I took back the brochure. That's when I saw that it wasn't just the list of words that someone had written on the flyer; someone had also circled information and had written some times in the margins. I studied them while I ate.

By the time I finished my first cookie, I was less grumpy. By the time I finished the second, I had an idea.

I looked at my watch. It was 11:14.

"Come on," I said to Clarence, standing up and wiping crumbs from my lap.

"Where are we going?"

"Nanu said no interrogating," I told him. "But she didn't say no spying."

Clarence thought it would be a good idea if I wore a disguise.

"The Dunstons don't know who I am, so it doesn't matter if they see me," he said, "but if they see you following them around, they might get suspicious."

It wasn't a bad idea, so I borrowed Nanu's big yellow hat from the coatrack, where she'd hung it to keep Matzo Ball from using it for a napping spot. I also grabbed her sunglasses from the entry table. They covered half my face.

On our way out the door, Nanu called from the kitchen, "Harriet! If you're going out, take Moneypenny along. She could use the fresh air!"

Moneypenny must have liked that idea, because she came right over and looked up at me eagerly.

Well, as eagerly as Moneypenny ever looks.

And so Clarence, Moneypenny, and I headed into town, to the pier. Where the glass-bottomed boats were docked.

According to the notes they had made in the brochure, the Dunston family had booked a ten-thirty a.m. ride on a glass-bottomed boat called the *Observer*. If we hurried, we might be able to catch them getting off the boat . . . and with any luck, we'd spot one of them carrying the Captain's binoculars.

Because it was a weekend, Marble Island was especially busy. A flood of tourists spilled through the village, most of them not paying any attention to where they were going. Some people looked down at maps; some were trying to rub on sunscreen while they walked, which meant they weren't doing either thing particularly well. I saw a man miss a whole big part of his arm. If no one told him, he was going to end up with a burned red stripe.

"Hey," I said, catching up with him. "You missed a spot."

"Oh," he said, "thank you."

Now that I'd done a good deed, spying on our guests felt less wrong. Like maybe this good thing evened out the kinda-sneaky thing of spying on people.

"Here it comes," said Clarence. He pointed out at the water. Sure enough, there it was, the *Observer*—a small green-and-white boat with a big green shade. I'd been on it a few times. People sat along the two sides and stared down at their feet. The whole bottom section of the boat was made of glass or clear plastic or something like that, so you could see fish and ocean plants and sometimes even sharks, but not the kind that bite. That's what Dad says, anyway, but I still wouldn't want to go swimming with them.

The good thing about wearing Nanu's floppy hat

and sunglasses was that I didn't have to shade my eyes with my hand to see out over the water. And then I noticed that Clarence's glasses had turned dark—that was pretty neat, how they could tell if he was inside or outside and change from clear to shaded, depending. I wanted to ask him how that worked, but the boat was docking. A teenage girl who wore a T-shirt that read "The Observer" in green block letters stood on the bow of the boat holding a rope, and as soon as it pulled close to the dock, she jumped off and tied the boat to a part of the pier.

"Come on," I said to Clarence. "Let's try to blend in over there." I pointed to a group of tourists on the pier who were taking pictures of a pelican perched on a post. A few of them were taking turns tossing sardines into the pelican's mouth, and everyone else was laughing and clapping and snapping pictures.

Clarence, Moneypenny, and I tucked in among

the pelican's fans. Clarence and I watched as people started disembarking—that's what it's called when people get off a boat. But Moneypenny's attention was on the wooden planks of the pier. She snuffed around and licked up every crumb she could find, like she was a vacuum cleaner. She was getting the pier so clean that I thought maybe the island should pay her or something. But then I figured that to Moneypenny, the crumbs were the reward.

"Do you see the Dunstons?" Clarence asked.

"Not yet."

"How about now?" Clarence asked, ten seconds later.

I shook my head. "Not yet."

Now the boat was mostly empty, and I was starting to worry that the notes on the pamphlet hadn't been made by the Dunstons after all. Moneypenny had snuffled clean all the wooden planks she could reach and she seemed totally tuckered out. With a sigh, she flopped onto her belly, her long, soft ear on my foot. I bent down and scratched her head.

I stood back up. I was about to tell Clarence that maybe we should give up and go home, but then the last group of people began to disembark.

"There's Senior!" I said, maybe a little too loudly, but luckily someone tossed another sardine into the pelican's mouth just then, and everyone cheered.

"Where?" whispered Clarence.

I pointed. "There."

Clarence pushed down my hand. "Don't point," he said. "That'll get attention."

I could have been annoyed at him for pushing my hand down, but he was right. We had to be careful.

Together, we followed the Dunston family up the pier, toward town, making sure to keep a group of people between us. (It hadn't been the easiest thing to get Moneypenny on her feet again. I had to pick her up and carry her for a little while before she'd walk on her own, and trust me, basset hounds are even heavier than they look.)

The whole Dunston family was together: Senior, Mr. Dunston, Mrs. Dunston, the teenagers Lilliam and Frank, and their older sister, Carmen. Every one of them wore a T-shirt that said something about who they were. Senior's said, "Grandfather of the Bride," Lilliam's said, "Sister of the Bride," and so on. Carmen's shirt said, "The Bride." It was sort of cute.

None of them was wearing the Captain's binoculars, but Mrs. Dunston carried a purse, and Frank had a big fanny pack that he wore across his chest, like a sash. The binoculars could have been in either one.

I knew from looking at the brochures that the Dunston family's next activity—kayaking—didn't start for half an hour. Maybe they'd grab a hot dog before they went over there. But they turned in another direction, and I knew exactly where they were heading.

Hans & Gretchen's Ice Cream Parlor.

When we got there, Senior was holding open the green Dutch door and waving everyone else inside, before following them.

"Come on," said Clarence.

"I can't go in there," I said. "Hans and Gretchen will recognize me for sure, even if the Dunstons don't. And besides, I don't think dogs are allowed."

"Well, I'm not going in all by myself," said Clarence. "People make me nervous."

"You've got to go in," I said. "When they get out their money to pay for the ice cream, you'll be able to see into at least one of their bags. It's our best chance to check for the binoculars."

"What would I do in there?" Clarence asked. "People don't just stand around in ice cream shops."

"Here," I said, reaching into my back pocket and pulling out my yard sale money. I counted out eight dollars. "Buy us each an ice cream cone."

The idea of ice cream seemed to make Clarence feel better about going inside alone. "What flavor do you want?"

"Vanilla." He headed for the door. "On a waffle cone," I called after him, in my loudest whisper.

A few minutes later, the Dunstons came back outside with their ice cream. I ducked behind a parked golf cart and crouched down, making sure that Moneypenny wasn't visible, either. She's probably the most recognizable dog on the island, and I didn't want her to give me away.

The family walked up the street toward Opal Cove, the best place to kayak if you want to see garibaldis. I didn't worry too much about them getting out of sight because I knew where they were headed.

It wasn't long before Clarence came out with two ice cream cones. He handed me the vanilla one. He had pistachio. "Where did they go?"

"Toward the beach," I said. "Did you see inside either bag?"

Clarence nodded. "I pretended I was looking at the ice cream flavors so I could get up close to the register. The mom opened her purse and dug through to find her wallet. She emptied like half the stuff onto the counter before she found it."

"Did you see the binoculars?"

He shook his head. "They weren't in her purse," he said. "I got a good look."

That was disappointing. Still, there was Frank's fanny pack. They could be in there.

And for now, there was this ice cream cone to finish. We ate while we walked in the direction of Opal Cove. Moneypenny kept up; she seemed to have gotten a second wind, or maybe she was hoping for some of my ice cream.

It was nice to walk down the sidewalk with a friend, and with ice cream. I was having fun, I realized. Lots of fun.

10

Orange Things, Big and Small

CLARENCE, MONEYPENNY, AND I HID behind some plants and watched the Dunston family strapping on life jackets and climbing into kayaks. I gave Moneypenny the last bite of my cone, the pointy bottom full of melted vanilla ice cream. She slurped it up in the curl of her tongue.

"If they recognize Moneypenny, the jig is up," Clarence said.

"That's what I thought, too," I answered.

"She needs a disguise," Clarence said, and he scooped up a handful of leaves and sprinkled them over her head and body. "There. Camouflage," he said.

Surprisingly, Moneypenny seemed to sort of like it. As soon as the leaves hit her fur, she stood perfectly still, like she wanted to keep them from falling off.

The three of us watched them push their kayaks into the water. When Senior climbed into his— long and orange and pointy at each end—it almost tipped over. But Frank and Lilliam steadied it and pushed him off before they got into their double kayak.

Even from behind the bush, I could hear them all laughing and talking as they paddled out into the water. I don't know why, but it made me feel *mad*.

Their shoes were in a pile down near the shore. But they'd left something else there, too.

Frank's fanny pack.

"Look," I said to Clarence, pointing.

"We can't go snooping through their stuff," he said, reading my mind.

"I know, I know," I said, even though I had been thinking about doing just that. "But . . . maybe it's not zipped up. That wouldn't be snooping, if it's open and we just look inside without touching it."

They were far enough away now that I didn't think they could recognize us onshore, not even Moneypenny. As if she agreed, she shook off the leaves, her long, heavy ears spinning like helicopter blades as she tossed her head. I started walking down to the sand, pulling Moneypenny along with me. The kayaks looked small, way out on the water. After a moment, Clarence followed.

"I think it's still snooping, even if the bag is open," he said.

Maybe he was right. Maybe he was wrong. Either way, it didn't matter. The fanny pack was zipped up tight.

We stood there, staring down at it. Nanu's hat flapped on my head in the breeze.

"I think it's too small to hold a pair of binoculars, anyway," said Clarence.

"Maybe they took the binoculars with them, out onto the kayaks," I said.

We turned and looked out onto the water. It was pretty—the sandy curve of the bay, the dark-blue water, the little orange and yellow kayaks, floating out there like pieces of fruit.

"If we had a pair of binoculars, we'd be able to see them better," Clarence said.

I looked at him, and he was grinning. That's when I started laughing, and then he did, too.

Then he said, "I'm hot. Let's put our feet in the water."

So we kicked off our shoes and peeled off our socks and I folded up my overalls until they were knee-high, and we waded into the water.

Moneypenny didn't protest; she must have been hot, too. She practically trotted into the water until she was chest-deep. Her ears floated like little boats.

The garibaldi probably thought we were there to feed them, which most tourists do, because they swarmed around us like giant goldfish.

"If you stand still, sometimes they'll suck your toes," Clarence said.

We dared each other to stand still, but it made me too nervous, waiting for a fish mouth to touch my foot, and I couldn't do it. Clarence couldn't either.

After a while, we saw the boats getting bigger again. "They're coming back," he said.

Even though we probably should have run back and hidden again, I couldn't move. I watched the way the kids and the parents and Senior all seemed to be having such a good time together, the way they were racing and laughing and splashing each other. As they paddled closer, I could hear the sounds of their voices but not the words, and I imagined what they were talking about—what a good day they were having, and how fun it was, and maybe what they'd eat for lunch.

It made me miss my mom and dad. But also, it made me realize how I was getting used to spending time here on Marble Island, and how in just another month or so, I'd be leaving to go home . . .

and then I'd be stuck missing Nanu, and Money-penny, and Hans and Gretchen's ice cream, and everything else here.

I didn't like that feeling.

I guess I'd been standing still long enough, thinking about all of that, to give those garibaldis their chance. Because the next thing I knew, I felt a weird sucking feeling on my big toe!

"Ahh!" I yelled, and I yanked my foot away. The fat orange fish darted off, looking for someone else's toe to suck, I guess.

"Hello, Harriet!" came a voice.

It was Senior, pulling up right next to me in his kayak. So much for my disguise. We were surrounded by the whole Dunston family. And not one of them was wearing the Captain's binoculars around their neck.

"Hello, Moneypenny," Senior added, and then, "Who's your friend?"

"Um," I said. "This is Clarence."

"Hello, Clarence," he said.

"It's nice to meet you, sir." For a spy, Clarence had excellent manners.

Senior's son, Junior—who was also Frank and Lilliam's father—said, "I like your hat."

"Thank you," I said. "It's my Nanu's."

Senior was wearing a hat, too. It was shaped like a bucket and it reminded me of the Captain's. I narrowed my eyes. "Where'd you get your hat?" I asked.

"Ah, that's Senior's lucky hat," said Junior. "He got it for a fishing expedition, what, Dad, twenty years ago? He has barely let it out of his sight."

"I caught twelve fish that day," Senior said. He looked happy just remembering. "Well, see you, Harriet. See you, Clarence."

They paddled to shore, and Clarence and I followed them. Our feet were too wet and sandy for shoes, so we just picked them up and shoved the socks inside.

"Look!" whispered Clarence.

I looked. Frank was picking up his fanny pack and unzipping it. He pulled something out—

A big orange nectarine. He took a bite. Juice dripped down his chin.

I sighed. "Come on," I said to Clarence. "Let's go back to the Bric-a-Brac. We can make sandwiches for lunch."

11

Shed Decorating

"AH," SAID NANU WHEN WE got back to the B and B. "There's my hat. And my sunglasses. I was looking for those."

"I didn't want to get a sunburn," I said. When you're as good at making things up as I am, you can sometimes do it without thinking. I bent down and undid Moneypenny's harness. She padded into the sitting room and flopped on the rug, as if she'd just finished a marathon. Which maybe she sort of had, considering the length of her legs and how far we had walked.

"Harriet," Nanu said, following us into the kitchen, "if you are going to borrow people's things, you need to ask permission."

"I'm sorry, Nanu. I'll remember to ask next time. We're going to make sandwiches."

Nanu stood in the kitchen doorway, holding her hat and sunglasses and watching me get out the bread and the jam and the peanut butter and two flat knives. Clarence spread the peanut butter, and I did the jam. I was glad to see Nanu had gotten more olallieberry.

When we were finished, I cut the sandwiches sideways to make triangles, and we loaded them onto plates. I got out a bag of potato chips, too. "We can eat outside," I told Clarence, and he went out through the back door.

"Harriet," Nanu said again, before I joined him.

"Just a minute, please."

I turned around. Nanu looked unhappy.

"I said I was sorry about borrowing your things without asking," I said.

"I know, Harriet, and I forgive you. But . . . is there anything else you might have borrowed, without asking permission?"

I didn't like where this was heading. "I thought you believed me about the Captain's binoculars," I said.

"Yes," said Nanu, "but, well, it does make me wonder a bit. If you should maybe think harder about whether you remember seeing the Captain's binoculars before the yard sale."

I felt a big hot bubble of mad rising up in my chest. If I were a garibaldi, I would have turned from orange to red.

"I'm not lying, Nanu," I said.

"Okay, Harriet, I believe you," Nanu answered.

But the look on her face told me that maybe that wasn't all-the-way true.

I went outside. Clarence was sitting at the iron table under the tree. His sandwich halves were still on his plate without any missing bites. As soon as I sat, he picked up the sandwich.

"Were you waiting for me?" I asked.

"Mm-hmm," he said, chewing.

That was a nice thing to do. I really liked Clarence. But that just made me think again about how I'd be leaving Marble Island in a month or so. It's hard not to get attached to people you like.

We ate our sandwiches in the shade of the tree. We listened to the tinkling wind chimes and munched the salty chips.

"What's that over there?" Clarence asked, pointing at the shed with his sandwich.

"That was Nanu's junk shed, but now that I cleared it all out, she says I can use it as a hangout."

"Really?" said Clarence. "Can I see?"

"Sure." I shoved the last of my sandwich into my mouth. I remembered to swallow before I said anything else. "It's got real windows and electricity."

We went into the shed. Clarence stood in the middle and turned in a slow circle, looking all around. At first I thought maybe he'd say something like "It's not very big," or "It's just an old shed," but after he'd finished his circle, he looked at me, pushed his glasses up his nose, and grinned. "This is awesome," he said. "Can I help you set it up?"

It turned out that Clarence knew a lot about decorating. He told me that the first thing we needed was a rug. "To ground the space," he said.

I had an idea where we could get one.

Mabel Marble was sitting on her back porch, working on a gingerbread house for the birds. She had all the supplies laid out on a table in front of

her—seeds and nuts and tweezers for moving them around, and a special glue she makes that's safe for birds to eat.

"Hello, Harriet," Mabel Marble said, looking up from her work. "Who's your friend?"

I guess I was inspired by Clarence's good manners, because I said, "Mabel Marble, this is my friend Clarence. Clarence, this is Mabel Marble."

"Hello, Miss Marble," said Clarence.

"Call me Mabel Marble," said Mabel Marble. "Everyone does. Would you two like to help me make fresh houses for the birds?"

"Maybe later," I said. "Clarence is helping me fix up the shed, and I wondered if maybe we could use the old rug you have rolled up in the corner of your kitchen."

"Ah," said Mabel Marble. "The rag rug."

"What's a rag rug?" Clarence asked.

"Bring it out here, and I'll show you," Mabel Marble said, so Clarence and I went inside.

He looked around at all the stuff—the stacks of dishes and the tablecloths and the bound-together newspapers. He stood there for a minute, just staring.

"C'mon," I said, grabbing one end of the rolled-up rug.

He grabbed the other, and we carried it out to the porch. Mabel Marble told us to untie it and lay it flat, so we did. And then we saw that the whole round rug was made up of little bits of cloth, tied and then braided together. I think every color that exists was in it, some bright, some faded.

"First you collect fabric," Mabel Marble said. "Old clothes, worn-out socks, tired dishcloths, anything will work. Then you tear the fabric into strips and sew them together into long strands. Then you braid the strands together, and then you're ready to shape the braids into a rug."

"That sounds like hard work," I said.

"Lots of things are hard work," said Mabel Marble. "That's no reason not to do them."

"We've got a whole pile of clothes at home that Dad says are too stained for us to wear anymore," Clarence said. "I wonder if I could make a rug out of them!"

Clarence didn't seem like a kid who was afraid of hard work. I liked that about him, too.

"Do you think we could use the rug for my shed?" I asked Mabel Marble.

She nodded. "As long as you let me come visit it from time to time."

"It's a deal," I said, and we shook on it.

Then Clarence and I rolled up the rug again and carried it across Mabel Marble's yard and through the gate, straight into the shed, where we laid it down.

"Wow," I said. "It already feels like a real room in here!"

"I told you we needed a rug," Clarence said.

I liked how he used the word "we."

By the time Clarence went home for dinner, we had managed to move in a card table and two chairs, my stack of books from the library and a couple of bookmarks, my rock collection (which I'd brought all the way to Marble Island from home), and Dad's miniature-making stuff. Clarence said most of the paint from the box I'd found in Mabel Marble's basement was dried out and useless, but I couldn't bring myself to throw it away.

After Clarence left, I spent some time arranging and rearranging the shelves. Then I decided to get Matzo Ball and show him the place.

He was snuggled up next to Moneypenny in their favorite sunny spot, the window seat. I almost felt bad about waking him. But I did anyway.

"Come on, Matzo Ball," I said, scooping him up by his fuzzy armpits. "I want you to see what I've been working on."

He was floppy and warm from his nap, and I buried my face in his peachy fur. He smelled like sunshine.

When we were in the shed, I turned on the light and closed the door so that he couldn't make a run for it and maybe climb over the fence into Mabel

Marble's yard, the way he'd done before. I love Matzo Ball, but I know from experience that he isn't trustworthy around birds. To him, they probably look like flying candy bars or something.

"What do you think?" I asked.

He skulked around in that funny careful way cats walk when they're in a new place and not totally sure about it. But after he sniffed most of the corners, he relaxed a little.

I sat in one of the chairs and opened a book where I'd left off, laying the bookmark on the card table. I read for a few minutes, but I was too excited about being in my new hangout to concentrate. Just think—it wasn't very long ago that the shed had been packed full of junk and I had found the old key in the chest of drawers, the key that led me to Mabel Marble.

Thinking about that made me think about the talk Nanu and I had had, the one when she told me that she used to steal things when she was young . . . like a pencil from a girl in her class who had better handwriting than she did.

A tingly feeling went up the back of my neck, making the little hairs there feel alive. Wait a minute. Nanu had confessed to me that *she was a thief* . . . was it possible that maybe *she* was the person who had taken the Captain's binoculars?

As soon as the idea came to me, I was sure it couldn't be true. There was no way that Nanu would steal the Captain's binoculars. Absolutely *no way*.

But one thing I knew about solving mysteries was that you aren't supposed to let *anyone* off the hook. If a person had the opportunity to be the thief, you are supposed to investigate them *no matter what*.

After all, sometimes in movies and books, the criminal is the person you'd least expect.

"Meow," said Matzo Ball, batting at the leg of my overalls.

"Not now, Matzo Ball. I'm thinking."

"Mrow," said Matzo Ball. He reached up with his fuzzy white-and-apricot paw and batted at the tassel of my bookmark, which was hanging off the edge of the card table. I put the bookmark back into the book and shut it.

"Okay, Matzo Ball," I said, picking him up and kissing him three times. "I'm getting hungry, too. Let's go inside."

I couldn't imagine why Nanu would take the Captain's binoculars. But if I was going to be thorough about solving this mystery, I was going to have to investigate Nanu, whether I liked it or not. While we ate dinner, I'd be watching her to see if there was anything she might be hiding.

12

Macaroni and Cheese and Marshmallows

UP IN OUR LITTLE APARTMENT we ate macaroni and cheese, but not the kind from a box. Nanu's
cheese sauce is homemade, and after she mixes it
into the noodles, she puts the whole thing in the
oven and bakes it until the top is brown and crispy.
Then she cuts slices out of it to spoon into bowls.

The corner pieces are the best because they have
the most crispy bits. This was something the Captain and I agreed on; she loves Nanu's macaroni

and cheese as much as I do. Whenever Nanu makes macaroni and cheese, the Captain joins us. So there were three of us sitting around Nanu's kitchen table that evening. The Captain is so tall that her legs filled up most of the space underneath the small, round table. She looked like she'd climbed into our dollhouse and was trying to fit in.

Moneypenny, who also loves Nanu's macaroni and cheese but knows she's not supposed to beg for it, lay down in her basket in the corner of the kitchen. Her long, spatula-shaped ears draped out of the basket and onto the floor. Watching as we ate, her mournful eyes followed each forkful.

"I think we should give Moneypenny her own serving," I said. "It seems sort of mean to torture her like this."

"People food isn't good for animals," the Captain said.

"I think Moneypenny would disagree," I said, disagreeing.

"That's the problem with people," the Captain went on, as if I hadn't spoken. "They want to turn pets and wildlife into people, instead of respecting the differences."

"Did something happen in the field today, Captain?" Nanu asked.

"Actually, yes." The Captain set down her fork. She pulled out her napkin—which she had tucked into her collar—and dabbed her mouth. "We were way out in Middle Ranch, where a big flock of island loggerhead shrikes has been nesting, and a deer came up to us in the truck, bold as can be!"

"Really?" That sounded exciting to me. "Was it cute?"

"It was adorable," the Captain said. "But that's not the point. The point," she said, picking up her fork again and stabbing a macaroni, "is that it wasn't afraid of us."

"Why would you want the deer to be afraid of you?" I asked. "If it were me, I'd be excited if a deer came right up to me like that." I jumped up and pretended to be a deer, using my hands to be its ears, and went right up to Nanu, sticking my face in hers. She laughed and kissed my forehead.

"That's the problem with people like you," said the Captain. "You and Mabel Marble and all the tourists. Making houses for birds out of seeds and nuts, feeding the deer marshmallows at the campground."

Maybe the Captain had more to say, but I had heard enough. I almost yelled. But then I remembered Clarence's good manners. So I said—in a not-yelling voice—"I don't know why you're so crabby, but there's no reason to be mean about it." Then I plopped back down into my seat.

"Oh, dear," said Nanu.

For a minute I didn't know if she was going to be mad at me for talking back to the Captain, even though I hadn't yelled, but then she said, "Captain,

I'm sure you've got quite a bit on your mind, and I'm sure it's distressing to see an emboldened deer. But surely you must want to apologize to Harriet for losing your temper."

Nanu didn't say it like it was a question. She said it like it was a statement. I decided to remember that, for later.

The Captain did look sorry. She set down her fork again, with the piece of macaroni stuck on it.

"Your Nanu is right," she said to me. "It's not your fault I'm upset. I am sorry."

I shrugged. I wasn't quite ready to forgive her, so I changed the subject. "Who's feeding marshmallows to the wildlife?"

The Captain sighed. She took off her glasses and set them on the table. "The deer that came up to us today had a jumbo marshmallow stuck to its ear. Picture that! A wet, sticky marshmallow caught up in deer hair. Some tourists down at the campground have been hand-feeding the deer and sharing videos of themselves doing it. It's become quite the trend to feed the wildlife. And that's not safe for anyone—not the campers, and certainly not the deer."

I thought about that. I could see that feeding marshmallows to a deer—as fun as it sounded—probably wasn't a great idea. Marshmallows aren't even good for *people* to eat, really. But what Mabel Marble did with her gingerbread houses seemed different.

We finished our macaroni and cheese, and we all did the dishes together, and then the Captain went downstairs. As we were putting away the casserole dish, Nanu said, "Harriet, I'm proud of you for speaking up for yourself. The Captain was short with you, and I liked the way you responded."

"You did?"

"Absolutely," said Nanu. "You were polite but firm. The Captain is strong-minded, and she is passionate about the things she loves. But some-times she can be brusque, and it's not your job to put up with that."

"What's 'brusque'?" I asked. I thought I had an idea of what Nanu meant, but I was enjoying this conversation, and I didn't want it to end.

"It means that the Captain doesn't always use gentle language or think about the impact of what she is saying. The Captain is a lot like you. Her intentions are good. But impact is just as important as intentions."

I didn't like being compared to the Captain. I guess there were times that I didn't think about the things I said, or the things I did. But it felt like as long as I didn't mean to cause trouble or hurt any-one with my lies, they didn't really count. I'd have to think more about all that.

Two things were for sure, I decided that night. The first, I thought as I put on my jammies and got ready for bed, was that Nanu really wasn't a suspect in the missing binoculars situation. She was too fair of a person to steal anyone's binoculars, even if she had stolen a few things when she was a kid. And she thought too much about other people's feelings to be hiding the fact that she had accidentally taken them, or something like that.

The second thing was something I thought about again when I went into the kitchen to collect Matzo Ball and found the Captain's glasses sitting on the table where she'd set them down. If the Captain could lose her glasses, she could most definitely lose her binoculars, too.

Nanu might not have had anything to do with the binoculars' disappearance. But the Captain might have. And that's who I'd investigate next.

13

Close Up

"HARRIET," NANU SAID, "THERE'S A package for you."

The next day, I was in the sitting room with Clarence. We were redecorating the dollhouse. First, we'd taken everything out, and we wiped the whole inside with soft dustcloths. It was dirtier than it looked in there. Then came the fun part: The Captain had given us a silver can of pressurized air with a long, skinny red straw stuck to the nozzle. Clarence and I took turns spraying air at the dollhouse furniture, blowing dust out of the little nooks and crannies.

Our plan was to turn the dollhouse's sitting room into a dining room and its dining room into a sitting room, and then decorate the whole place for a birthday party. In real life, the island was getting ready to celebrate Mabel Marble's centennial birthday, and since the dollhouse was modeled after her real house, it seemed like it should be decorated. We were going to make streamers out of strips of paper towels that we had dyed with food coloring, and we had some little yellow pom-pom balls I'd found in Nanu's sewing bag that we were going to try to make look like balloons.

While we were decorating, we went through our list of suspects, though we had to whisper about it because Nanu was just in the next room. I told Clarence that I'd eliminated Nanu, and he agreed that she couldn't be the thief.

"After all," he whispered, "her whole job is to make the B and B guests happy, and stealing her longest-staying guest's binoculars would be the opposite of making her happy."

The Dunstons were still suspects, and so was the Captain. It wasn't a very long list, but we were stuck on what to do next to continue the investigation.

Anyway, that's what we were doing when Nanu told me there was a package for me. It was a small-ish, flattish rectangular box. "Harriet Wermer" was written on the front, along with the address for the Bric-a-Brac B&B.

It was in my dad's handwriting.

I opened it. There was a folded note, which I put inside my book to read later, and then I tipped out the heavy thing inside. It was an odd shape, and it was wrapped up tight in newspaper. I unwrapped the newspaper, too.

"It's my dad's magnifying glass!" It seemed like a bit of *serendipity*, which is a fun-sounding word

that means "uncommon luck." (I learned that word from the Captain.) When Dad had visited, he'd said he would send me the magnifying glass so I could look more closely at his miniatures; neither of us had known then that, by the time it arrived, I'd be in the middle of an investigation.

I held it up so Clarence could see it. It had a black handle and a silver rim and the glass was shiny and polished. I looked at Clarence through it. He looked huge.

"Neat," Clarence said.

"He promised to send it so I could see all the little screws and nails in the dollhouse furniture." I picked up a miniature dining room chair and held it under the magnifying glass. Too close to the glass, it was blurry, but when I moved it away a little bit, it got clearer. I could see how Dad had attached the legs to the base; a tiny, dried drop of yellow glue mushed out from where the leg connected with the underside of the seat.

"Wow," I said. Not about the glue or the chair. Just . . . that my dad had held this little chair, just the same as I was doing, lots of years ago, before I was even born, when he was just a kid. And this tiny, dried drop of yellow glue was proof of that. It was evidence.

"Harriet, have you seen the tiny tablecloth?" Clarence asked.

I shook my head, but I wasn't helping him look for it. I was too busy trying out Dad's magnifying glass. I picked up the red dollhouse couch and flipped it over. Looking through the magnifying glass, I could see the tiny nails Dad had used to build it.

Clarence went over to the armchair where Matzo Ball was curled up.

"There it is. Matzo Ball, give that back," said Clarence, trying to unhook the little piece of fabric from Matzo Ball's claws.

"Meow," said Matzo Ball.

We set up the dining table in front of the fireplace. It looked like a cozy place to eat a meal.

"I've got to go home for lunch," Clarence said after we'd gotten all the furniture in place. "Don't decorate the rest of the dollhouse without me, okay?"

"Okay," I said.

"Promise?"

I held up the magnifying glass and looked at Clarence through it. He grinned.

"Promise," I said.

• • •

After Clarence left, I wandered through the bed-and-breakfast, looking at things through the magnifying glass. Things are different, close up. I peered at Nanu's yellow hat, and through the magnifying glass I could see Matzo Ball's leftover fur, and also that the fabric was woven out of individual threads. This got me wondering if all fabric is made that way, which got me looking at all the other fabric I could find: my overalls (yep); the dishcloth draped over the edge of the kitchen sink (yep); the velvet pillows on the couch (yep).

Pretty much everything I looked at through the magnifying glass had more to it than it seemed.

"Harriet," Nanu called from the kitchen, "what are you doing?"

"Looking at things," I answered.

"Ah," said Nanu. She came into the dining room, where I was examining the curtains. "Find anything interesting?"

Through the magnifying glass, I could see that the threads that made the curtain fabric were made of tinier threads that looked like little strands of colorful hair. "Everything is interesting," I said.

"That's my girl," said Nanu proudly.

I wandered into the backyard, still carrying the magnifying glass. I looked at the cluster of flowers near the back steps. They were light violet with yellow middles. Through the magnifying glass, I saw that the yellow stuff looked light as fur, and little pieces of it dusted the insides of the violet petals, too. I saw the way the petals folded a little at their bases, where they attached to the center of the flower. And I saw that the yellow stuff on the green stems—that I'd always thought was the same as the yellow stuff in the middle of the flowers—was actually hundreds of little tiny bugs! They were alive, and I think one of them looked back at me.

"Will you look at that," I whispered to myself.

The bugs climbed over one another, a mess of tiny antennae and tiny legs.

I heard the kitchen door open and close. "Nanu!" I said. "Come look at these bugs. There's a million of them!"

"Aphidoidea," said a voice behind me. Not Nanu's—the Captain's. "Commonly known as aphids. One of the favorite snacks of chickadees and wrens. Good eye, lass."

The Captain squatted next to me. She peered down her nose through her glasses at the bugs—I guess Nanu had returned them to her.

"That's quite an infestation," she said.

"Are they good for the garden, or bad?" I asked.

"Both," said the Captain. "They suck sap from the plants, and they leave behind a residue, which can lead to mold. That's bad. But other insects—like ladybugs—love to eat aphids, and once ladybugs

come to eat aphids, they'll stick around and eat other pests, as well. That's good. Things aren't always all good or all bad, lass. Nature is more complicated than that."

I thought about what the Captain had said after she went back inside, about things in nature being more complicated than all good or all bad. I knew that was true about things other than nature, too.

Like having to spend the summer on Marble Island. That was bad, because I missed Mom and Dad. But it was good, because I had met Mabel Marble and I'd set up the shed all cozy, and I had a new friend. But it was also bad again, because we still hadn't found the Captain's binoculars, and I knew she thought I had something to do with their disappearance, even if she wasn't talking about it anymore.

There was only one way I could think of to find out whether the Captain had misplaced the binoculars herself the day of the yard sale, and that was to follow her around and see if I could spot any clues about where she would have set them down and forgotten about them. Maybe if I paid very careful attention to everything she did, I'd see things more closely—just like with the aphids. So, dusting off the knees of my overalls, I followed the Captain back inside.

14

You'll *See*

MAYBE IT'S BECAUSE THE CAPTAIN'S job is to watch things—island loggerhead shrikes—or maybe it's because the Bric-a-Brac B&B is too small for spying. But it only took the Captain about three minutes to notice that I was following her around.

"I already have a shadow, lass," the Captain said when she caught me following her up the stairs to the second floor. "I'm not in need of a second. Is there something you want?"

"I'm not following you," I lied. "I'm just heading in the same direction."

"Ah," said the Captain. We'd reached the second-floor landing. "Where are you going?"

"Up to my room to get something."

"Ah," said the Captain again. "What do you need to get?"

"Playing cards," I said. I don't know why I said that.

"Aren't those kept in the cabinet in the sitting room?"

"Oh," I said. "I forgot."

The Captain stared at me like she was about to say something else, but then she didn't. She turned and headed up the hallway toward her room. She went inside and shut the door. I waited a minute to make sure she wasn't coming out, and then I tiptoed after her, avoiding the squeaky spots on the floor.

When I got to her door, I took Dad's magnifying glass out of the loop on the side of my overalls. I think the loop was meant for carrying a hammer, but the magnifying glass fit just right. I didn't really know what I was looking for, but I looked anyway. I looked at the wood trim all around the door. I looked at the little table in the hallway, where the Captain stashes the things she takes into the field with her. I'd seen her binoculars on this table lots of times, along with her notebook and her camera and her extra socks. I didn't need the magnifying glass to examine this stuff, but I used it, anyway. Wouldn't it be funny, I thought, if somehow the Captain's binoculars were sitting right here on this table, and no one had noticed?

I imagined it so clearly that I could practically see it happening in my head. I pictured myself finding the binoculars and then knocking on the Captain's door, and the look on her face when she opened the door to see me standing there holding them, and the way I would tell her, "I told you I didn't take them!"

I got myself so convinced that I would find the binoculars sitting there that when I didn't, I almost didn't believe it. I had to look three times before I accepted that the binoculars really weren't there. I stuck Dad's magnifying glass back into the loop on my overalls and headed downstairs.

"There you are, Harriet," said Nanu. She was in the sitting room, rearranging pillows and putting odds and ends into the cabinet. "It's time to get ready for afternoon tea. Will you give me a hand?"

"I can't give you a hand," I said. "I need both of them. But I can loan you a hand." I grinned at my own joke.

"Good enough," Nanu said, smiling back.

I sort of like tidying up, especially at the Bric-a-Brac, where everything has a place that it belongs. The dollhouse furniture goes in the dollhouse (I just piled everything together in one dollhouse room, since I'd promised Clarence I wouldn't decorate without him). The puzzles go in the puzzle cabinet. The books go on the bookshelf. The magazines go in the magazine rack.

And the island brochures get lined up in stacks on the side table. I restacked each stack, tapping them straight. "There," I said, satisfied.

Matzo Ball was turning in circles on the Captain's favorite thinking chair, getting ready to give it a good scratch. I don't like telling Matzo Ball what he can and can't do, but since the Captain had been in such a bad mood about the cat hair and the clawing and the bird chasing, I decided maybe it would be better if Matzo Ball found something else to do. I picked him up and carried him over to the sunny spot on the floor.

That's when the Dunstons came back from whatever they'd been doing. Senior had thick white sunscreen in a line across his nose, and all of them looked a little worse for the wear, as Nanu liked to say. By which I meant they were all a little worn out from spending too much time in the sun.

"Just in time for tea," Nanu said cheerily, and Mrs. Dunston said, "How lovely! We'll be ready in just a few minutes, after we clean up."

Frank and Carmen and Lilliam all trudged up the stairs, and Senior headed for the downstairs bedroom. But Mrs. Dunston and Mr. Dunston hung back, like they were waiting for everyone else to leave before they spoke to each other. I don't know why, but it seemed to me that maybe one of them was about to say something important, so I pretended to be very busy dusting the bookshelf. One thing I've noticed is that if you look very busy doing something, it's almost like you're invisible.

When there was no one left in the sitting room besides me, Mr. Dunston whispered to Mrs. Dunston, "We've managed to find something old, and something new, and something blue. But we still need something borrowed."

"Don't worry about that," Mrs. Dunston said. She was whispering, too. It made it sound like they had secrets. Suspicious ones. "I've taken care of it. You'll *see*."

Mr. Dunston smiled and nodded, relieved. "You really are the best," he said to Mrs. Dunston, and the two of them *giggled*. It's not often that you hear grown-ups giggling.

Then they left the room, and I stopped pretending to dust. The back of my scalp was itchy with an idea. Had it been my imagination, or had Mrs. Dunston said, "You'll *see*," rather than "You'll see," as if the word "see" was extra important?

Binoculars are used for seeing. What if the thing Mrs. Dunston had borrowed was the Captain's binoculars? It didn't seem likely . . . but it wasn't impossible. After all, if she'd "borrowed" them for something other than sightseeing, she wouldn't have taken them out on their excursions yesterday. If she took them for the wedding tradition that Clarence had mentioned, then she would have hidden them.

I needed to know more. And then, noticing how the dining room was set up for tea, I got an idea.

I looked at my watch. I only had a little while before teatime. Maybe not *enough* time. But there was only one way to know for sure.

15

A Tour of the Wood

I COULD BARELY TALK WHEN Jamal opened the door of 43 Aster Place, and I had a cramp in my side from running.

"Harriet?" he said. "Is everything all right?"

"I need . . ." I breathed in and out hard. "Clarence!"

"Okay," Jamal said. "Come on in. I'll get him for you."

He left the door open and walked down the hallway toward Clarence's room. I was too out of breath to take another step, and I put my hands on my knees while my heart banged around in my chest.

It felt like forever, but it couldn't have been more than a minute or two before Clarence came to the door.

"Harriet?" he said, sounding just like his brother. "What are you doing here?"

"C'mon," I said, grabbing his hand. "We've got spying to do!"

The good thing about Clarence was that he seemed to understand when something was an emergency. He didn't ask questions; he just ran with me back to the Bric-a-Brac B&B. We took the stairs two at a time and then stopped outside the yellow front door. If we were breathing that hard inside the house, there was no way we'd be able to be sneaky enough to pull off my plan.

I told my heart and my breathing to *slow down*, and after a minute, they did. Then I held my finger up to my lips and Clarence nodded, understanding. Slowly, I turned the doorknob, hoping to find the downstairs rooms empty. If teatime had already started, we'd be too late.

The sitting room was empty. So was the dining room. Its table was covered with tea stuff—teapots and cups and saucers, the sugar bowl and cow-shaped cream pitcher, the three-tiered rack of finger sandwiches (100 percent finger-free, as Nanu liked to say), and scones. Underneath all the tea stuff was Nanu's long pink tablecloth. The one that reached almost all the way to the floor. This used to be her second-favorite tablecloth, but now that Matzo Ball had ruined the blue one, I guess this one was her favorite.

I tiptoed to the desk in the corner of the dining room where Nanu kept the spare keys to the guest rooms. Very quietly, I slid open the drawer. There was the ring of keys.

"Harriet," Clarence whispered. "What are we doing?"

"The guests are going to be having tea in a few minutes," I whispered back. "They'll all be distracted. We can go look in Mr. and Mrs. Dunston's room. I heard them say something suspicious!" I reached my hand toward the key ring. My fingers were shaking.

"Harriet, stop," hissed Clarence. "I don't think this is a good idea. This doesn't feel fun, like down at the beach. We can't break into their room!"

I blinked. Clarence knew how important this was, and if one of the Dunstons had the binoculars, did it really matter how we investigated it? I was going to ask him just that, but then I heard people starting to come down the stairs. We were too late. I shoved the drawer closed and looked around. "Quick!" I said, turning back to the table. I dropped to my knees and lifted the tablecloth. "Under here!"

I crawled under the table, and Clarence followed. The tablecloth dropped behind us, and just in time.

As soon as we were under the table, I realized there was no reason for us to hide; we could have just joined everyone for tea! But by then, it was too late.

The Captain was first to arrive, which was no surprise. She was always hungry. I could tell it was her by her shoes; they were brown leather with thick soles, good for hiking. Her shoelaces were double-knotted.

"Ho-ho," came her voice, sounding pleased. "Two kinds of scones today!" There was a clattering over our heads as the Captain picked up a plate and loaded it full. I'd seen her at enough teatimes to be able to imagine her plate—it would have two or three scones in the center, each topped with a wallop of clotted cream and jam, and five or six finger sandwiches shoved in around the sides. After she'd piled the plate, she'd set it on the table—sure enough, there was a clattering overhead—as she poured herself "a bracing cup of tea." I heard the stream of tea hitting the bottom of the teacup, and the sound of it made me want to use the bathroom.

Then I heard another clatter as she stacked the plate of snacks atop the teacup, and then her sturdy brown shoes turned on their heels as she went into the sitting room to eat in her thinking chair.

Then came Nanu, clomping loud as a pony as she pushed through the swinging kitchen door. Her purple clogs had rounded leather toes and wooden soles—that was what made all the racket. Her shoes came toward the table and then stopped beside it. Sometimes Nanu liked to stand near the table during teatime in case the guests needed anything. I hoped she'd leave this time, though. I didn't think the Dunstons would talk about the binoculars if Nanu was there to hear, and as long as we were hiding anyway, maybe we would overhear something useful.

Then I heard uneven footsteps from up the hall and saw what had to be Senior's shoes—black leather, shiny, with a hard square heel and a bunch of little holes poked into the leather over the toes in a fancy pattern. His shoelaces were black and thin, tied and then tucked in so that you couldn't see the bow.

Then came Mrs. Dunston, in bright-pink high-heeled sandals. I don't think I'll ever understand high heels. The only thing they'd be good for is reaching things on a high shelf.

"Hello, Senior," Mrs. Dunston said. "Care for a scone?"

"Don't mind if I do." His pointed shoes stepped closer to the table, the tips of them underneath the tablecloth, dangerously close to my knees. I tried to breathe as lightly as I could. I could feel the shape of Clarence next to me, and I felt him doing his very best not to move a muscle. The whole thing was mostly scary but also a little bit funny.

"I'll get more cream for the tea," Nanu said. "Back in a jiffy." Clomp, clomp went her clogs, as she went back into the kitchen.

Next to me, Clarence leaned into my arm, like he was trying to get my attention, but I kept staring straight down at the tips of Senior's shoes. I was afraid that if I even turned my head, Senior or Mrs. Dunston would hear me.

"These look delicious," said Senior. Then he lowered his voice and whispered, "So, I hear you've got something borrowed for us."

"It's true," whispered Mrs. Dunston. "I can't wait for you to *see* it." That time, the emphasis on "see" was undeniable. She *had* to be talking about the binoculars! Was she whispering to keep the Captain from overhearing?

Clarence pulled at my sleeve, and he was pointing at something in the sitting room—the Captain, maybe? I couldn't tell, but now wasn't the time for a distraction. I shook my head and put my finger over my lips again.

From the staircase came a rush of footsteps—and then two pairs of shoes. The fancy high-top sneakers, extra large, had to belong to Frank, but it took me a minute to figure out if the sandals were Lilliam's or Carmen's. It was the toenails that helped me solve that mystery; the big toe on each of Carmen's feet was polished with "Mrs." in white cursive letters.

"Would you care for some jam with your scone?" Mrs. Dunston asked Senior hurriedly, as if she didn't want Frank and Carmen to wonder what they had just been whispering about, which made her sound even more suspicious.

I couldn't think about that for very long, though, because right then someone else arrived. The worst possible someone else.

First we heard the clickety-clackety of her claws on the wooden floor. Then we saw her big old snout poking its way under the tablecloth, sniffling and snuffling.

"Shh, Moneypenny," I whispered as quietly as I could. "Go away!"

But Moneypenny wasn't going anywhere. Her mouth opened and her tongue lolled out, almost as long as her spatula-shaped ears, and then she shoved her whole head under the table and *licked*

my face, a big, warm, slimy trail of dog spit all the way up my left cheek.

"Moneypenny, what are you doing under there?" asked Nanu, pushing back through the swinging door and into the dining room, and then it wasn't just Nanu's clogs I could see anymore. I could see the tops of her socks . . . and then the bottom of her skirt . . . and then she was kneeling on the floor, lifting the tablecloth, and I could see her whole face. I wanted to squeeze my eyes shut to make her disappear, but I knew that wouldn't really do any good, so instead I yanked my magnifying glass out of the hoop on the leg of my overalls and peered up at the bottom of the table and said, "You see, Clarence, all the different textures in the wood? I told you it looked different on the bottom than on the top."

"Um," said Clarence.

"Harriet?" said Nanu. "Clarence?"

"Oh, hi, Nanu," I said, my voice as cool and

casual as a cat. "I was just showing Clarence all the different types of wood we have here in the bed-and-breakfast. Clarence is really into wood. Aren't you, Clarence?"

"Um," said Clarence again. I shoved him with my elbow. "Oh," he said. "Yeah. Mahogany especially. And acacia."

"Acacia," said Nanu, raising an eyebrow. "Well, why don't the two of you conduct the rest of your wood tour later, after teatime?"

She motioned with her chin for us to get out from under the table, and we did. Moneypenny, the old tattletale, licked Clarence's legs as he clambered to his feet.

"All right, Harriet, Clarence. How about if you get a snack, and then later you can help me clear the dishes."

Nanu turned back to her guests. I grabbed a plate.

It was embarrassing for spies to get caught like

this, but maybe we wouldn't get in too much trouble, especially if Nanu believed my lie about the wood.

"Harriet!" whispered Clarence. No one looked over at us. They'd all returned to their scones and tea.

"Harriet!" he whispered again, a little louder this time.

"What, Clarence?" I didn't really feel like talking. I just wanted to get a scone and go hide in a corner somewhere and figure out how I was going to find out what the Dunstons had borrowed.

"The binoculars," Clarence whispered. "I know where they are!"

16

The Plot Thickens

I MANAGED TO STAY CALM. I poured a glass of lemonade for Clarence and another for myself, and we got a few finger sandwiches. Then I said, "Hey, Nanu, we're going to go have our snack in the backyard."

She had a suspicious look on her face, but she didn't try to stop us. It wasn't until we were on the back porch with the door safely closed behind us that I said, "Well? Where are they? Did one of the Dunstons have them?"

I caught Clarence with a bite of cream-cheese-and-cucumber finger sandwich in his mouth, so I had to wait until he chewed and swallowed to hear his answer. I'm not very good at waiting, and I could feel myself getting itchy on the inside of my skin, all anxious and excited.

Finally he said, "I was only able to see them because we were under the dining room table, so close to the floor. Because they are under something, too. They're under the couch in the sitting room."

That didn't make any sense to me. Who on earth would have gone through all the trouble of stealing the Captain's binoculars, just to hide them under the couch? I remembered what Mrs. Dunston had said about "taking care" of the "something borrowed" for the wedding. Shoving them under the couch didn't sound like she was taking care of them at all.

So if the Dunstons hadn't taken them and put them under the couch, who had?

"We should go inside and tell the Captain where her binoculars are," Clarence said, finishing his second finger sandwich.

"No," I said, and maybe it came out kind of rude and bossy.

Clarence froze. "No?"

"We can't tell her yet," I said. "If we give the binoculars back to the Captain without examining them for clues, we might never find out who took them in the first place. And if I don't have proof of who did it, she and Nanu are probably going to assume I took them and just waited to give them back until it seemed like it wasn't me!"

"But," said Clarence, "isn't it kind of dishonest to know where they are and not say anything?"

There was that word again. Dishonest. "Look, Clarence." I used my stern voice. "I know you're the one who found the binoculars, but I'm the one who started the search for them. And I'm the reason that we were under the table, and you never would have seen the binoculars if we hadn't been. So it's up to me to decide when to tell the Captain, not you."

Clarence turned away from me, and as he turned, the sun caught and reflected on his glasses so they looked like little patches of shine and I couldn't see his eyes. He sat that way for a minute, and there was

a feeling between us that I didn't like but couldn't exactly name.

Then he said, "Whatever, Harriet," and he stood up. "Tell your Nanu that I said thanks for the snacks." And with that, he walked around the side of the bed-and-breakfast and through the gate, and then he was gone.

I opened the back door. Nanu was doing dishes at the sink, and so I got on my tiptoes to sneak past her. If she saw me, she might ask me to help, and this was my chance to go fish out the binoculars and examine them for clues. But the sitting room wasn't empty; Mrs. Dunston and Senior were still there.

I stopped in the dining room and stood very still, listening.

"I can't wait for the rehearsal dinner tomorrow night," Mrs. Dunston was telling Senior. "We can finally show Carmen what we've gotten her! I still remember how, when I married your son, you gave me your 'something blue' . . . that lovely velvet ribbon for my hair."

I snuck one eye around the doorframe to see what Mrs. Dunston was doing. She was reaching into her oversized bag.

"Meow?" Here was Matzo Ball, choosing the worst time to want to play. He pushed his forehead against my leg and began to purr.

First Moneypenny, and now Matzo Ball! It was like some sort of a pet conspiracy. I tried to ignore Matzo Ball. Sometimes if you refused to make eye contact with him, he got bored and walked away. But other times, he took it as a challenge. Unfortunately, this was one of those times. He stood up on his hind legs and whacked at me, trying to get my attention. His claws were so sharp that I could feel them even through my denim overalls. He is the cleverest and cutest cat in the world, even if he's sometimes sort of annoying.

"Ooh, I *see* what you meant! It's perfect," Senior said.

Then Mrs. Dunston, looking past Senior, said, "Harriet, are you interested in what we're going to be giving to Carmen tomorrow evening?"

I guess I wasn't being as sneaky as I thought. I felt my face blushing bright red. I picked up Matzo Ball and I stepped into the sitting room. "I was just . . ." I tried to come up with an excuse for why I'd been spying on them, but I couldn't think of anything to say.

"Look," said Senior, turning. And in his hand was . . . a bracelet.

I stepped closer. It was a delicate silver bracelet, with tiny white pearls and little pink seashells all strung together. And then I understood—Mrs. Dunston hadn't been saying "You'll *see*." She'd been saying "You'll *sea*."

"The whole wedding is ocean themed," Mrs.

Dunston told me. "Carmen loves the water so much that she's practically a fish! And your grandmother was kind enough to loan this to us. Isn't it perfect?"

"Oh," I said. "That makes a lot more sense."

"A lot more sense than what?" Mrs. Dunston asked.

I just shrugged. "It's a pretty bracelet," I said. "Carmen is going to love it."

Then Mrs. Dunston went upstairs and Senior went down the hall to his room. I was alone in the sitting room, except for Matzo Ball, who I set down on the Captain's thinking chair, and Moneypenny, who was sleeping on the couch.

I took a quick look around. No one was coming. So I flopped onto my belly and reached under the couch, fishing around. My fingers brushed something—a strap. I pulled on it—

And then they were in my hands. The Captain's binoculars.

But as I got them out from under the couch and started to sit up, that's when Nanu decided to come in from the kitchen. I shot up and whipped around to face her, my hands holding the binoculars behind my back.

"Harriet," she said, "what's that you're holding?"

"A seashell," I said, which is maybe the dumbest lie I ever told. Nanu held out her hand and, reluctantly, I pulled the binoculars from behind my back.

"Oh, Harriet—" she began to say, but before she could finish, she flipped them over, and the two of us saw the same terrible thing.

One of the lenses was cracked, all the way down.

"Oh my," said Nanu.

And then there were footsteps, coming down the stairs. Again, I recognized the loud march of leather shoes—the Captain.

"Agnes," said the Captain, "you found my binoculars!"

"Actually," Nanu said, turning to me, her face full of disappointment, "Harriet had them."

She handed the binoculars to the Captain, whose face fell when she saw the cracked lens. I remembered then what she'd told me. That the binoculars had been a gift from her father. Without thinking, my hand went to the weight of the magnifying glass in my overalls loop.

"Harriet," the Captain said, and there was so much disappointment in the way she said my name, the same disappointment I'd seen on Nanu's face.

"I didn't do that," I said, but even as I did, I could tell how it sounded. I had a bad, sick feeling in my stomach.

"Harriet," the Captain said again. "It's one thing to accidentally break something. But it's another thing to lie about it and hide the evidence."

I opened my mouth. I closed it. I felt as wordless and floppy as a fish. I turned to Nanu. *She'd tell the*

Captain what was what, just like she had at dinner last night.

"Harriet," Nanu said. "Is there something you'd like to tell us?"

Well, the feelings that welled up inside me were like a terrible storm. Like churning water out at sea and waves crashing up against cliffs and thunder and lightning inside my chest. I was mad.

I crossed my arms. I stomped my foot. "Yes," I said. Maybe I yelled. "I *do* have something to tell you. I wish I'd never come to Marble Island in the first place. I wish I was home, where people *believe* me when I tell them the truth."

I stormed right out of the front door, slamming it behind me. I wanted the weather outside to match my mood, but the sky was beautiful and the breeze smelled like flowers. *Nothing* was going my way.

I stomped to Clarence's house and banged on the door.

After a minute, it opened. "What do you want, Harriet?" he said.

Well, this certainly wasn't the friendly welcome I'd expected. "I got the binoculars out from under the couch. They were right where you said they were."

Clarence blinked, but he didn't say anything. So I continued. "The thing was, one of the lenses was broken. And then Nanu and the Captain saw me holding them, and they blamed me for breaking them. You need to come back over, okay, so we can figure out how the binoculars got under the couch, and so we can find the person who broke them and prove that it wasn't me."

Clarence didn't come outside. He didn't open the door wider to let me in, either. He didn't look sorry for what had happened to me. He didn't say how awful it was that the Captain and Nanu were blaming me for the broken binoculars. Instead, he said,

"I don't think I want to hang out anymore, Harriet. Good luck with everything, okay?"

I couldn't believe what Clarence was saying. It wasn't okay. Not even a little bit okay! I wanted to tell him how wrong he was, and how he couldn't just stop hanging out with me.

But for once, when I opened my mouth, nothing came out.

Clarence stepped back into his house and closed the door.

17

A Nightmare

I DON'T KNOW IF YOU remember this about me, but sometimes I have really bad nightmares. So bad they are called night terrors. And usually, they are about falling.

That night, I had one of those terrible dreams.

In my dream, I was in the dollhouse. I don't know how I knew I was in the dollhouse; I just *was*. I was in the sitting room area that Clarence and I redecorated, and I was taking a nap on the little couch. Only it didn't *feel* little to me. It felt regular-sized, which meant that I was little.

Anyway, I was taking a nap on the couch in the sitting room of the dollhouse, and for a blanket I was using the tablecloth that Clarence had been looking for. It was pulled all the way up to my chin, and I was pretty comfortable. But then, all of a sudden, this enormous curved razor-sharp *knife* tapped me on the knee. And then, suddenly, there were five of them, and they hooked into the tablecloth-blanket, pulling it slowly down, and I was all wrapped up in it, so I was being pulled down, too, and I was falling, and falling, and—

Thump! I woke up, tangled in my blanket and sheet, on the floor of my bedroom at Nanu's place. Matzo Ball looked down at me from his perch on my pillow, where he was still tucked into kitten position. "Meow," he said, and that is when I had a terrible, terrible thought.

I put the blanket and sheet back on the bed, even pulling the blanket around Matzo Ball so he would be nice and warm. I put on my overalls over my pajamas, tucking Dad's magnifying glass into the loop on the leg, and checked to make sure the flashlight on my watch was working. Then, slowly, carefully, I cracked the door to my room.

Nanu had left a stack of my laundry outside my door, which was nice of her. It made me feel worse about the sneaking around I was about to do.

The thing about a big old house like the Bric-a-Brac B&B is that it has what Nanu likes to call "quirks." That means that some parts of it aren't the way you would expect them to be. Like, the top stair leading down from Nanu's apartment to the second floor is about twice as big as the next step down, so you've got to be prepared for it. And the handrail makes a funny groaning sound if you lean too hard on it, and there are squeaky spots both on the stairs and on the floor.

When you're living in an old house, you have to get to know it. That's just the way it is. And even though I'd spent lots of time at the B and B all throughout my life, and even though I'd been living here for the whole first part of the summer, there were things about the Bric-a-Brac that I still didn't know.

That's how I got surprised by the doorknob on the closet door on the second floor. I've walked past that doorknob lots of times. But I'd never noticed that it sticks out more than the other doorknobs! In fact, I don't think I'd ever noticed that doorknob at all until right then, when I was trying my best to be sneaky and quiet, tiptoeing down the hallway, paying attention to every squeaky floorboard, and doing my very best not to wake up any of the guests.

That's when I ran right into that doorknob with my hip.

I don't mind telling you that it hurt pretty bad. And it wasn't the quietest thing ever, either. But even though I wanted to yelp, I managed to keep my mouth shut tight. I froze in place, waiting for one of the guest room doors to open. If they hadn't heard me run into the doorknob, I was sure that everyone on the entire second floor must be hearing the loud pounding of my heart.

But the doors stayed closed. I let out my held breath as gently as I could. Then I made my way to the Captain's door.

I'd been worried that she wouldn't have put her binoculars on the little table where she sometimes leaves them, but there they were. It was dark in the hallway, and I needed to take a close look at the binoculars to see if my suspicions were correct, so I pressed the button on my watch to turn on the flashlight. A bright white beam of light cut through the shadows. I aimed my wrist at the binoculars on the table. The flashlight beam shined against the cracked lens, but that wasn't what I was here to examine.

I pulled Dad's magnifying glass from the loop in the side of my overalls. I held it to my eye. I shined the light at the binoculars' black nylon neck strap. Slowly, I examined the whole length of it.

And then—there. Exactly what I'd hoped I *wouldn't* find. Proof that my hunch about the culprit was right.

Fang marks. And loose threads, pulled out by long, sharp claws.

I knew exactly one creature who could do that sort of damage. Who would pull something off a table and drag it under the couch. And right now, he was sleeping in kitten position on my pillow.

I'd wanted to solve the mystery of the missing binoculars to prove that the Captain was wrong about me . . . and to make her admit that maybe she was wrong about Matzo Ball, too.

But if the Captain found out that Matzo Ball was the culprit, then she'd believe more than ever that she was right about him being a problem. I remembered what the Captain had said—"Something must be done about that cat."

Just then, the Captain's door swung open, and there was the Captain. She was wearing light-blue pajamas with yellow duckies all over them; her metal-gray hair stuck up in all directions. I might have thought that it was funny to see her like that if I hadn't been so shocked and scared.

"Harriet?" she said. "What are you doing outside my door in the middle of the night?"

I knew what I had to do.

I switched off the flashlight on my watch. I put my magnifying glass back into the loop on my overalls. I drew myself up as straight and tall as I could. I looked the Captain right in the eyes. And I said, "I'm here to confess."

18

The Confession

AS SOON AS I TOLD the Captain that I was there to confess, she said, "Hold on, lass. Let's head upstairs and get your Nanu. Middle-of-the-night confessions shouldn't take place standing up."

As we were going upstairs, Nanu came hurrying down, her gray and white and silver and brown curls a big mess from sleeping.

"Harriet, there you are," she said. "What on earth are you doing out of bed at this hour?"

"The lass has a confession," the Captain told Nanu. "I thought it would be best to hear it together."

Nanu must have seen from my expression how upset I was. She said, "Let's go upstairs and have a nice warm cup of something. Shall we?"

I followed Nanu, and the Captain followed me. In Nanu's apartment, the Captain put her binoculars on the kitchen counter, and Nanu set out a platter with cookies. Then she poured milk and chocolate into a pot and heated it on the stove. When it was ready, she poured three mugs of steaming hot chocolate and set them on the small round kitchen table. Then she said, "Why don't you tell us all about it, Harriet. We are listening."

She tightened the belt on her fuzzy pink robe and sat down next to the Captain, who was still wearing her duckie pajamas.

I guess Moneypenny got woken up by the sound of the three of us, because she wandered in slowly, stopping halfway through the doorway to give a big yawn. Then she flopped down under the table and went back to sleep.

I picked up one of the mugs and brought it close to my face. The dollop of whipped cream was beginning to melt into the hot chocolate, just the way I liked. I took a sip even though it was still too hot, to buy some time. I had to think of a good lie, fast.

I don't know about you, but I don't usually plan to lie. What usually happens is this: things aren't going the way that I want, or I'm bored, or I'm anxious or crabby or mad, and I open my mouth and the lie just sort of *happens*. Like when I told my dad that going to Doug's Drive-Thru De-Lite for smoothies was a last-day-of-school tradition, even though there was no last-day-of-school smoothie tradition. I don't think I told him that lie because I wanted a smoothie all that much. I think I was just upset that Dad was picking me up from school instead of Mom, like I was expecting. I'm not really a fan of things not going the way I expect. So then I lied about the smoothies.

Honestly, the lies I sometimes tell surprise *me* more than anyone else. I'd never really thought before about why I lie. But right then, I did. And I thought that usually, when I make up a lie, it's to distract me from a scary truth about what is happening or what I'm feeling. Because the truth is sometimes scary. And lying makes me feel in control.

But this time was different. This time, I *needed* to lie. And I needed Nanu and the Captain to believe my lie so that the Captain wouldn't hate Matzo Ball.

It was a lot of pressure.

Nanu and the Captain were waiting for me to finish my sip and explain myself. I heard the soft padding steps of Matzo Ball, coming to join us in the kitchen, and I saw him come through the doorway.

Then I set down my mug. It was time to lie.

But when I opened my mouth, a lie didn't come out. Not exactly. Instead, I said, "It's my fault the binoculars were missing, and it's my fault they got broken."

And that wasn't a lie, not really. Actually, it was the truth! Matzo Ball was my cat, and my responsibility. If I hadn't insisted on him coming with me to the island, the binoculars never would have gotten broken.

I hoped that maybe they would just accept my confession, and then I'd get in trouble, and that would be that. No one would ever have to know that sweet Matzo Ball was the culprit.

But that's not what happened. Instead, Nanu said, "Harriet, we're going to need a bit more explanation than that. Why would you have taken the Captain's binoculars in the first place?"

"Umm," I said, "it was because of how great the Captain is always making the island loggerhead shrikes out to be. She makes such a big deal of how important they are, and how interesting they are, and how clever they are, and I was starting to feel left out that I'd never seen one in real life. The Captain said that she'd take me to look for them when I was able to be quiet for a whole half hour, but I didn't really see that happening anytime soon."

All of that was true, about the shrikes—I really did want to go bird-watching for them with the Captain. A lump formed in my throat as I wondered if she'd ever take me bird-watching now.

"Hmm," said the Captain. "Where did you find the binoculars in the first place, lass?"

That one was easy. I didn't even have to lie. I swallowed the lump in my throat and said, "You'd left them sitting downstairs on the side table again."

"I don't leave my binoculars on the side table," the Captain said.

"Actually," said Nanu, "I find them there quite often. I take them upstairs and place them on the table outside your door."

"You do?" said the Captain, looking a bit embarrassed.

Nanu nodded

"Well," said the Captain, and she cleared her throat. "Thank you."

"All right, Harriet," said Nanu. "Let's get on with it. How exactly did the binoculars get broken?"

"Yes, Harriet," said the Captain. "Let's hear the rest of the story."

Both Nanu and the Captain were looking at me with all their attention. Neither of them was drinking their hot chocolate.

Well, they asked for it. If they wanted a story, I'd come up with one. A really good one.

"So," I went on, "I took the binoculars and I headed outside. Not into the backyard. Mabel Marble's trees are full of birds, but not island loggerhead shrikes. I went into the front yard and down toward the beach."

"Meow," said Matzo Ball from behind me, over

near the counter, but I ignored him. I was on a roll now.

"The shrikes aren't big fans of surf and sand, let alone crowds of people," said the Captain. "Good luck finding any of them at the beach."

"Exactly," I said, nodding enthusiastically. "I looked all over the beach, using your binoculars, and I didn't see a single shrike. Though I *did* see a pelican on the pier, catching anchovies that tourists were throwing to him."

"Those tourists," the Captain said, going a bit red in the face, "always feeding the wildlife. Don't they understand—"

"There, there," said Nanu calmly. She nudged the platter in the Captain's direction. "Have a cookie."

The Captain tucked a napkin into the collar of her pajama top and selected a cookie. She took a bite.

"So, I gave up on the beach. And then I thought of the perfect place to look for shrikes in town. Over by Hans and Gretchen's Ice Cream Parlor. There's the big oak tree, with the grassy area beneath. Maybe there would be some shrikes nesting in that tree. So, I went over there, and I looked through the binoculars, right up into the branches and the leaves. And then I saw something moving!"

Nanu sat forward in her chair. "Was it a shrike?" she asked.

The Captain seemed distracted. She was looking at something behind me. If I was going to keep her attention, I'd have to make the lie even more exciting.

"I thought it might be a shrike," I said, "until an acorn crashed through the leaves and smashed right on the lens of the binoculars, cracking it. A squirrel threw it down, straight at me! The binoculars probably saved me from being hit in the eye if you think about it. Anyway, as soon as that happened, I rushed straight back to the B and B and hid the broken binoculars under the couch."

The Captain was looking at me now, with a strange expression on her face. She picked up her mug and took a sip.

"And that," I said, "is my confession. I'm sorry I took your binoculars without permission. I'm sorry I broke them. And I'm sorry I lied about it."

"Well," said the Captain, pulling the napkin out of her collar to wipe off a whipped-cream mustache, "that's quite a confession, lass."

I thought so, too. "So," I said, "do you believe me?"

"I believe that you really love your cat," the Captain said wryly.

"What does *Matzo Ball* have to do with anything?" I asked, maybe a little too loudly.

The Captain nodded at the counter behind me. I turned and looked.

There was Matzo Ball, reaching up with his cute fuzzy paw, claws extended, batting at the binoculars' neck strap, which hung down from the counter. He just about caught it, too, and was about to pull it over the edge. I jumped up and ran across the kitchen.

"Matzo Ball," I whispered, "cut it out!" I grabbed the binoculars just in time.

"I have a different theory about what happened," said the Captain. "Do you want to hear what I think?"

"No," I said, at the same time that Nanu said, "Yes."

"Here's what I think happened," said the Captain. "I think that a very distractible ornithologist left her valuable and special binoculars lying around downstairs with the strap dangling off the side of the table, instead of putting them away safely. And then I think that a fluffy peach-colored cat did exactly what cats do best—he hunted them. And he tugged them to the floor, breaking the lens, and then he pulled them under the couch, where they stayed until you finally noticed them."

I didn't have anything to say to that.

"Oh, Harriet," said Nanu. That was all she said. But she didn't sound angry, or disappointed.

My eyes were full of tears. I put the Captain's

binoculars on the table, making sure that the strap wasn't dangling. Then I slumped back into my chair. "Are you mad?" I managed to ask, around the lump in my throat.

"Well," said Nanu, "I *was* a bit distressed to think that you were gallivanting around the island, all alone. But no. I'm not mad."

I looked at the Captain. Through the tears in my eyes, it looked like there were two of her. Then I blinked, and the tears spilled, and there was just one Captain. And she didn't look mad, either.

"The big mystery," the Captain said, "is why you didn't think you could trust me."

At first, I just shrugged, miserably. But then— something changed. Not only did I not want to lie—by omission or any other way—I wanted to tell the truth. A bigger truth than what happened to the binoculars. A truth I hadn't been fully aware of until just then.

"Captain," I said, "I know you don't really like Matzo Ball, and I know you don't really like me. But . . . I like you. I think you're smart and interesting and I like the way you wear things with lots of pockets rather than things that look good. I like that you wear practical shoes and double-knot the laces. I like that you love animals, even more than you like most people. I even like that you're so particular about the things you like, and, well . . . I thought that if you knew the truth about Matzo Ball, you would like him even less. And you'd want to send him away because of how much trouble he is." I felt my throat get tight and my eyes get hot and wet. "And I'm a lot of trouble, too."

"Oh, lass," said the Captain, and Nanu said, "Oh, Harriet," but she said it differently than before. She didn't sound disappointed; she sounded sad.

"First things first," said the Captain. "Thank you for the nice words about my clothes and shoes and for saying that you think I'm interesting. That's high praise, coming from someone as interesting as you."

I sniffed and wiped my nose with the sleeve of my pajamas.

"And, for better or worse," the Captain said, "you remind me a bit of another lass I know. One who was curious, and opinionated, and grew up to be an ornithologist."

She folded her napkin and handed it to me. I dried my tears.

"Now. Why on earth would you think I wanted to send your cat away?"

"Because," I said. I could feel myself starting to cry again. I hate crying. "Matzo Ball gets his fur everywhere and claws your thinking chair and he chases birds whenever he gets outside and you kept saying that something had to be done. Like sending him away."

A strange look came across the Captain's face. "Stay right there, lass," she said. "I'll be right back." She stood up and went downstairs.

"Meow," said Matzo Ball. Maybe he knew we were talking about him. He is the world's smartest kitty. He jumped onto the table and came over to my face. He bumped his forehead on my forehead, which is a cat's way of saying "I love you."

The Captain was on her way back in a flash. I could always hear her before I could see her. She came into the kitchen and set something on the table, in front of me. It was brown leather, rectangular, and it had a zipper that went around three sides.

"Open it," she said.

I pulled the zipper across the top, down the side, and across the bottom. Then I could fold it open like a book.

Inside was the fanciest cat grooming kit I'd ever seen.

There were silver claw clippers and a flea comb with a wooden handle and brushes in three different sizes. There was a round natural sponge and a small soft cloth and a glove that had little nubs all over the palm, for massaging.

"Did you buy this for Matzo Ball?" I could hardly believe it.

"Of course I did," said the Captain. "We have to take care of our family, don't we?"

Family. Back home, my dad and mom and Matzo Ball were my family—and soon my baby brother would be, too. But here—here my family was Nanu, and Matzo Ball, and lazy old Moneypenny . . . and the Captain, too, I now knew. I wasn't going anywhere, and neither was she.

"This is really nice," I said. "Thank you."

"Well, it's enlightened self-interest," she answered. And then she unzipped a little pouch on the back of the grooming kit and pulled out a shiny silver cat collar, with a shiny little bell on it. It made a pretty tinkling sound when she shook it. "This should give the island birds a bit of a warning, if he gets outside again."

"And," I said, "Matzo Ball will look so handsome in silver."

The Captain cleared her throat and said, "Listen up, lass. I'm sorry I didn't believe you in the first place."

I shrugged. "It's okay. I understand why you didn't. I've been trying really hard not to lie. And I'll try harder."

"Okay," said the Captain. "And I'll try not to leave my things lying around, tempting Matzo Ball and making more work for your Nanu. And tell you what. If I hear you spinning a yarn, I'll let you know you slipped up so you can make a different choice. And if you see me being forgetful with my things, you let me know, too. Deal?"

She stuck out her hand. It was a big hand, tanned

dark from all the time she spent outside, sort of
leathery. I shook it. It was strong and warm.

"Deal," I said.

"Now," said Nanu, "who's going to help me finish off this hot chocolate?"

"Me," I said, and so did the Captain, at exactly
the same time. And then we laughed together, and
we shared it fifty-fifty.

19

Close Up, Far Away, and Just Right

THE NEXT MORNING, I WOKE up early. Super early, early enough that Matzo Ball was still tucked into kitten position on my pillow, early enough that on the second floor, I could hear the Captain snoring in her room, early enough that on the ground floor, Nanu wasn't making muffins and coffee yet. I went out to the front porch and watched the sky change from violet to pink to day colors. I listened to the birds waking up and telling each other all about everything. I sat there for a long time, until I saw the island waking up in front of me, and heard the B and B waking up behind me.

I wanted to all-the-way enjoy it. I wanted to enjoy the sky and the birds and the wide wooden front porch. But I knew I couldn't. Not until I made things all-the-way right. So I went down the porch steps, and up the street, and around the corner.

When I got to the doorstep of 43 Aster Place, my stomach was flipping and flopping. Even still, I knocked.

Clarence answered. Before he could say anything—or maybe even shut the door in my face, which I would sort of deserve—I started talking, fast.

"I was a jerk," I blurted at Clarence. "I was pushy and I acted like a bully and I didn't listen when you told me you were uncomfortable and I sort of made you lie. But that's not who I am."

I was talking too loud. I was practically yelling. That was because I wanted so badly for everything to be okay between us. But . . . I couldn't *make* Clarence forgive me. I couldn't yell him into agreeing to be my friend. If I wanted to set things right, I was going to have to be all-the-way honest. Even if it was really hard. And what I'd just said to Clarence wasn't the whole truth.

"Actually," I said, more slowly now, and quieter, "I guess those things sort of *are* who I am."

Clarence's forehead had little wrinkles across it, like he was thinking.

I went on. "But those things aren't *all* of who I am. And they're not the way I want to be. I'm really sorry, Clarence. And that's the truth."

Clarence's forehead relaxed, and he blinked.

I held my breath, waiting. I decided I'd stand and wait as long as it took. For Clarence, I could be quiet for thirty whole minutes, all in a row. Even more, if he needed me to.

It didn't take thirty minutes, but it took a while. Finally Clarence said, like he really was curious to know, "What's the way you do want to be?"

"I want to be friends," I said. "Real friends. The kind of friends who listen to each other and trust each other and don't try to be in charge and are patient with each other. And tell the truth." I did want that. I really, really did.

I think Clarence could tell that I meant it. He nodded. "Okay," he said.

When I got back to the Bric-a-Brac B&B, the Captain was sitting on the porch step. She had Matzo Ball on her lap! She was brushing his coat with one of his new brushes in long, slow strokes, and she murmured, "Aren't you a pretty boy? Such a pretty, pretty boy."

Matzo Ball purred loud as a motor. And I was right; he did look handsome in his new silver collar.

"Good morning, Captain. Good morning, Matzo Ball," I said.

"Hello, lass," the Captain said. "You're up early."

"I've had something important to do, and I didn't want to wait a minute longer."

The Captain nodded approvingly. "A girl after my own heart," she said.

Sometimes, it's good to see things close up—the way Dad's magnifying glass helps you do. And sometimes, it's good to see things far away—the way the Captain's binoculars help you do (when they're not broken).

But sometimes, you don't have to see super close up or super far away. Sometimes, what's exactly in front of you, natural and easy, is enough.

That's how it felt around the B and B after we found the binoculars, and after the Captain and I made our promise to help each other remember our goals—me, to stop lying, and her, to stop leaving things around. It felt natural and easy. Just right.

Later that week, after we said goodbye to the Dunston family, Mabel Marble invited us over to help with a new project. She wanted to make a gingerbread birdhouse for every house on the block before her birthday at the end of the summer. "I want to celebrate turning one hundred years old by making the whole neighborhood of birds happy," she told us.

When the Captain grumbled about feeding the wildlife, Mabel Marble said, "Well, the wrens and chickadees sure seem to love my birdhouses! They come to visit me every single day, just about."

"Wrens and chickadees?" I said. "Captain, didn't you tell me that those are the birds that most like to eat aphids?"

"I did, lass," said the Captain. And later I heard her asking Mabel Marble if we could maybe take one of the birdfeeders back to the Bric-a-Brac. "We could use a few more feathered friends on our side of the fence," she said. "The aphid situation over there is looking a bit grim."

I was helping the Captain hang our new gingerbread birdfeeder near the violet-and-yellow flowers when Nanu came outside, holding the phone. The long pink cord was stretched tight from the wall in the kitchen. "Harriet, dear," she said, "it's for you. It's your dad."

"Just a minute," I said, "I'm holding the ladder for the Captain."

After the Captain had the birdhouse hung in the tree and had climbed safely down, I took the phone from Nanu.

"Hi, Dad," I said.

"There's my girl." Dad's voice sounded so close that he could have been standing right next to me. But he wasn't.

"Are you and Mom and the baby okay?" I asked.

"Mom and the baby are doing great," said Dad. "The doctor says the baby is getting big and strong, and as long as your mom keeps resting, there's no reason to think he'll be born early."

"That's good news," I said.

"It's the best news," Dad answered. Then he

said, "Harriet, did you get a chance to think about what I wrote?"

"What did you write?" I asked.

"In the note that I sent with the magnifying glass," he said.

"Oh," I said. I had totally forgotten to read the note. I'd been so excited about the magnifying glass that I'd folded Dad's note into my book and then I never read it.

A lie was on the tip of my tongue. I almost said something like "I read your note and I'm still thinking." But then I glanced over at the Captain, and I saw the way she was picking up all the little bits of twine left over from hanging the birdfeeder, which she normally might have forgotten about. And so, instead of lying, I said, "Dad, I completely forgot to read your note. I'm sorry. I'll go get it right now."

"Oh—" Dad said, but I set down the phone and ran into the B and B to find the note.

It was right where I had left it, in a book on the table. I pulled it out and read it.

Dear Harriet,
Mom and I hope you are still having a great time with
Nanu and Moneypenny! And I hope you'll see lots of
neat stuff through my old magnifying glass.
Things are changing a bit for me as far as work
goes . . . it looks like I might be laid off. Nothing to
worry about! But it means you could come home early if
you want, instead of staying with Nanu until the baby
is born. Why don't you think about it, and let us know?
Love,
Dad

Carefully, I refolded the note. Slowly, I went back outside to where I'd left the pink telephone receiver.

I picked it up, but I didn't put it to my ear just yet.

Instead, I thought about what I was going to say.

Not that long ago, I'd told Nanu and the Captain that I wanted to go home. But now that maybe I could, I wasn't so sure that that was really what I wanted anymore.

"Harriet?" I heard Dad's voice coming through the phone. "Are you there?"

I lifted the receiver to my ear. "Hi, Dad," I said. "I found the note. I read it."

"Okay," said Dad enthusiastically. "Well, what do you think? I could come and get you the day after tomorrow, if you want."

"Um," I said. "I don't think I could be ready quite that soon."

"No problem," said Dad. "I could come the day after that, if it would be better."

I swallowed hard. This wasn't going to be easy. "Dad," I said at last, "don't be mad. But . . . I think I want to stay at the B and B this summer. The way we planned."

"You do?"

I nodded. "It's just . . . well, I made a friend. His name is Clarence."

"Harriet! That's fantastic!"

"Yeah," I said, feeling better now. "He's really great. And the Captain promised that as soon as the new lens comes for her binoculars, she'll take me and Clarence out to the middle of the island to search for island loggerhead shrikes. I still haven't seen one, and they sound really neat. And there's the centennial celebration for Mabel Marble's one hundredth birthday . . . I can't miss that. Hans and Gretchen are counting on me to help them test flavors for the ice cream cake they're going to make. And the B and B is a lot of work for Nanu, all on her own. She says I'm a big help."

"Harriet," Dad said, and he sounded like maybe he was going to cry.

For a minute I was sorry I'd told him the truth. What if I'd hurt his feelings? What if I'd hurt his feelings *so bad* that he was going to be mad at me, or disappointed?

But then he said, "Harriet, it sounds to me like you're doing great. As much as Mom and I miss you, it seems like you are right where you need to be. I'm proud of you."

I grinned. "Thanks," I said. "I'm proud of me, too."

"Harriet," the Captain called from the garden, "good news!"

"I've got to go," I said into the phone. "But I'll call you soon. Okay?"

"All right, Harriet. I sure do love you."

"I love you, too," I said.

I hung the phone on the hook in the kitchen. Then I went back into the yard. The Captain was on her knees in the flowerbed, peering closely at a flower.

"You have that spyglass?" she asked.

I nodded. Dad's magnifying glass was hanging

from the loop on the side of my overalls, just like always.

"Take a look," the Captain said, raising her chin in the direction of the flowers.

I lifted the magnifying glass to my eye. There on a green leaf was a shiny red bug, covered over with black freckles. "It's a ladybug," I said.

"*Coccinella septempunctata*," said the Captain, wisely. "Commonly known here in North America as a ladybug. And a ladybird across the pond."

"What pond?" I asked.

"The Atlantic Ocean, Harriet," said the Captain. She sounded stern, but I knew her well enough now to recognize that this was just her science voice. "And I'll give you one guess about what our fine freckled friend here likes to eat."

"Aphids," I said, remembering.

"Exactly," said the Captain. "I'll tell you what I think we should do. We should get ourselves a whole swarm of these cute little beasties. Between the ladybugs and the birds, those aphids don't stand a chance. What do you think?"

My first thought was that I sure was glad the Captain and I were on the same side of things. My second thought was: "You can buy ladybugs? Like from a store?"

"Oh, sure," said the Captain. "I've got a bug guy." She stood up and brushed dirt from her knees. "Let's go inside and help your Nanu get the tea on, and I'll tell you all about him."

"Do you think there are any cookies left?" I asked, hoping.

"If there are," said the Captain, "you can bet we'll find them." Then she reached out her big, weathered, rough hand. Not for me to shake. For me to hold.

And we went hand in hand up the steps, through the door, and into the Bric-a-Brac B&B, where Nanu was waiting for us.

Acknowledgments

When I was a kid, I really, really wanted to be a published author. Like, more than anything (except maybe having my very own horse). But when I looked at books on library shelves, I was filled with despair: I knew I could never do that.

It turns out I was correct. What I didn't know is that no writer creates a book alone. I write a manuscript—a flawed, imperfect, burgeoning book-to-be—and then a whole team of people helps it become the book you are holding in your hands.

That team includes friends—in this case Martha Brockenbrough and Nina LaCour, who read the manuscript several times; Rubin Pfeffer, who always offers support and insight; Jordan Brown, my editor, who really knows how to shape a mystery, and how to gently push in the right directions; artist Dung Ho, who drew the book's fantastic cover art and interior illustrations; and the team at Walden Pond Press / HarperCollins, including Debbie Kovacs, Christian Vega, Donna Bray, Molly Fehr, Amy Ryan, Emma Meyer, Lauren Levite, Jessica Berg, Annabelle Sinhoff, and Jennifer Sale. I am grateful to you all.